Blood Brothers

BOOKS BY THE AUTHOR

The River's Edge
Thomas Francis Meagher and Elizabeth Townsend Meagher;
Their Love Story
Annie
The Cabin In The Woods
Forever Friends
No Time For Tears
Under the Banyan Tree
Blood Brothers

Books are available from Primix Publishing
Co., websites and bookstores.
Books may be ordered by contacting the author:

Lenore McKelvey Puhek
1215 Hudson Street
Helena, MT 59601
E-mail: lpuhek@gmail.com
Telephone: 1 406 443-2552

Blood Brothers

MONTANA TERRITORY 1860 - 1890

Lenore McKelvey Puhek

Primix Publishing
11620 Wilshire Blvd
Suite 900, West Wilshire Center, Los Angeles, CA, 90025
www.primixpublishing.com
Phone: 1-800-538-5788

Published by Primix Publishing   02/28/2022

ISBN: 978-1-955177-96-2(sc)
ISBN: 978-1-955177-97-9(e)

Library of Congress Control Number: 2022902515

Contents

Chapter 1 1
Chapter 2 7
Chapter 3 9
Chapter 4 11
Chapter 5 14
Chapter 6 18
Chapter 7 21
Chapter 8 27
Chapter 9 28
Chapter 10 32
Chapter 11 35
Chapter 12 40
Chapter 13 45
Chapter 14 50
Chapter 15. 59
Chapter 16 62
Chapter 17 67
Chapter 18 70
Chapter 19 76
Chapter 20 81
Chapter 21 86
Chapter 22 89
Chapter 23 93

Chapter 24 101
Chapter 25 107
Chapter 26 111
Chapter 27 119
Chapter 28 123
Chapter 29 127
Chapter 30 129
Chapter 31 131
Chapter 32 136
Chapter 33 140
Chapter 34 145
Chapter 35 150
Chapter 36 154
Chapter 37 157
Chapter 38 161
Chapter 39 163
Chapter 40 166
Chapter 41 169
Chapter 42 176
Chapter 43 182
Chapter 44 186
Chapter 45 190
Chapter 46 194
Chapter 47 198
Chapter 48 202
Chapter 49 205

Dear readers:

In the last half of the 1860's approximately 25,000 Blackfoot Indians were in the Montana Territories. During this time various tribes fought over 1500 skirmishes against the Union Army. The tribe kept being pushed west by more powerful tribes.

Forts provided a safety net for the Western movement of homesteaders and city builders. The Civil War was winding down; soldiers had no place to go and were willing to chance a new life.

Signed Peace Treaties allowed access to the Indian trails. It is said the gold rush was the main reason for coming west. However, for most it was a desire to start over in a new location; develop a farm, raise a family, design towns and businesses. It also brought the rich and the curious. Last but not least, the movement provided hiding places for outlaws. We label this period of history as the "romance" of the West with cowboys and cattle drives. It allowed a new freedom from the already over-populated cities in the east. The admonition of the day came from Andrew Greeley who shouted, "Go west, young man, go west."

My book is a novel based on historical facts. It is not a chronological history of the Blackfoot tribe. My purpose is to set down insights into the Wild West. Angry letters, sent from homesteaders who had been led to believe the West was a safe place to begin a new life, alerted the government leaders that protection from the Indian tribes was necessary if there was to be an expansion.

My story peeks into the tipi of Bear Chief, the Blackfoot leader who was forced to put his people on the reservation near Glacier National Park. How vision quests directed his decisions. One major event that killed nearly 10,000 Blackfoot people was the introduction of a white man's illness called Small Pox. Infested blankets brought up river and given as gifts to the Blackfoot was only one of the various ways to try and annihilate the Native American Nation. There were Indian Schools funded by the government who boarded thousands of Native Americans. An example of their intention comes from the Carlisle Indian Industrial School's motto: "Kill the Indian; Save the man."

My purpose is to educate present day Americans about the early days of the West. Today over seventy percent of the Native Americans speak English.

⸻ ◆◆◆ ◆◆ ◆ ⸻

He watched with half-shut eyes as three young braves crossed the Missouri River at the edge of camp, their ponies moving slowly. Earlier that morning Bear Chief had walked toward the river bank to say his morning prayers to the rising sun, just as these same eight-year-old boys plodded softly through the waist-high grasses. He did not make any signs to the boys, pretending not to notice them. The boys did the same. He knew they were looking his way by the tilt of their heads. He also knew they were afraid of their great chief and this made Bear Chief smile.

In the late evening hours this same scene reversed itself as the boys made their way back to their tipis and family. They jostled each other, using narrow willow sticks for spears as they pretended to count coup. Laughter usually announced their return and Bear Chief stood near the river, looking stern; his arms crossed over his breast plate, and when he thought of it, he'd wear his fancy eagle feather head-dress. He looked strong and very scary to the respectful boys.

These boys, around eight years old, handpicked by Finds the Elk, were strong and quick to learn. Their training this day was to keep the village horses penned in a roped moveable corral, seeing to it that the animals went to the river to drink. Their job was to be fast and keep the herd together. Older, more experienced men rode the night shift, keeping away wild wolves, mountain cats and human predators. They wore quivers full of arrows over their shoulders. Some of the men carried rifles and were excellent shots with the fire-sticks if and when needed. For a warrior to take a horse in coup brought him many favors. Owning horses was a sign of wealth as well.

Bear Chief's achievements in his younger days advanced him through layers of training knowing he would someday lead this tribe. Like his father before, now gone to the Sand Hills, the villagers needed leadership and authority. Times were hard.

White men, called blue-coats, lived at the confines being built out of mud squares at Fort Shaw. A Medicine Man had come to Bear Chief many years ago to tell him that he saw a war in a vision. The Plains tribes would be in many more wars. A white man known as Yellow Hair would bring trouble.

Bear Chief shook his head. His hair had not been cut since he was born over twenty-five seasons ago. That one small curl of black hair had been tied with a leather thong, along with a piece of sage. His mother had placed the items inside his sacred medicine bundle. Every morning he went through the ritual of allowing his hair to be free; to blow in the wind.

This morning, however, Bear Chief awoke stiff and aching. It had been a long, bad night for both him and Flower Woman. He stretched his legs, bent his knees and swung each leg forward and backward. He shook his hands. Then he drew in a long, deep breath and began chanting. Soon he would dance in a circle. While walking he prayed to the Great Spirit and thanked Him for keeping his village safe: his warriors, woman; animals, four-legged and two-legged alike; for the blessings of wild berries and meat. He thanked the Great Spirit for their good health. Bear Chief's mind would not stay on his prayers. He stopped his dance. *I must wait…wait for a sign…what sign?*

He spent the afternoon planning for the gathering of the many tribes that would bring hundreds of family here to his camp. They would powwow as well as pray for peace with the white man.

A Peace Treaty allowing the white man to pass through Indian country on certain trails had been signed earlier that spring. Many had not obeyed the Treaty. A band of renegade Blackfoot warriors were being accused of burning buildings and destroying planted crops of the homesteaders. Every day the commander at Fort Shaw heard another complaint about the Blackfoot band stealing horses; stopping wagons and destroying their load that homesteaders needed to work the land. Bear Chief shook his head. *How can I make them understand they must follow the Treaty? We cannot fight the white man flowing into this Valley. All must go well for at least the five days we are in camp.*

In preparation for the feasting and dancing, Bear Chief had hunters looking for antelope, deer, ducks, dogs, pheasants, geese, chickens, as his cooks would need meat. The women had already told him what supplies they needed from Bent's Fort. Bear Chief shook his head again. *Much fire water will flow during the rendezvous when the mountain men arrive.*

The men would expect an empty tent to play the stick game. Guards wandering throughout the camp would try to keep the drunken men from fighting one another. Maidens would be in a circle, step-dancing around a huge bonfire at night, wearing fancy costumes trying to entice young Braves to dance with them. *I need Flower Woman's help and she is not able to be at my side.* She and her boy-child, son of Bear Chief, were to be given a ceremonial welcome. There would be no ceremony; there was no boy-child.

Bear Chief's runners made smoke-talk to him every afternoon. He had not sighted any smoke this day, even though the sky was blue; the wind still. That was not a good sign. Surely the tribes were moving closer each day. The Peace Treaty allowed passage through the country.

As evening approached, Bear Chief watched for the returning boys. He did not hear their laughter when he saw them riding their ponies bareback. He heard splashing river water as the ponies carefully made their way to the other side, stopping very close to Bear Chief's tipi. The boys stayed on the ponies waiting for permission to dismount.

Bear Chief looked at each boy. "Come to me."

Two boys slid off their mounts while Wise Owl sat the pony. He called for his friend, Comes At Dawn who moved quickly to Wise Owl.

"Take this bundle to Bear Chief."

Comes At Dawn reached up and grabbed the bundle wrapped in calico cloth. Bear Chief heard a faint cry. Still he did not move from his place guarding the entrance to his tipi. His woman slept inside and he didn't want her disturbed by this intrusion.

Bear Chief nodded and motioned the boy to come forward. He glanced to the right side of the tipi and walked into the shaded area.

Comes At Dawn followed. The bundle was quiet once again. The other boys stood frightfully still as statues, watching as the Chief carefully unwrapped the cloth.

"What! What is this?" Bear Chief stepped back and stared at Comes At Dawn.

"Were did you find this infant?" No one spoke. Bear Chief lifted the naked baby, covered in feces and blood, towards the sky. "This is not a Blackfoot child. He is a white man's child; brown eyes, brown hair, white skin."

Much to Bear Chief's surprise, the baby kicked his scrawny little legs and arms. His cry seemed louder than before, as if the infant demanded to be fed; to live. Someone, probably his mother, had severed the umbilical cord. A sharp rock would easily cut them apart.

Bear Chief pointed his finger at "Wise Owl. Come to my tipi after you eat. Leave now. Tell no one."

Wise Owl was afraid. "Can I tell Looking Back? She will wonder why I am late for her meal."

"No." Bear Chief said, "Tell no one."

Happy to escape the stares of Bear Chief, the frightened boys jumped back onto their ponies. One swift kick in the ribs sent them galloping towards the river. The full moon, hidden behind a bank of dark, ominous clouds, slipped across the blackened sky. It only took a few minutes for the boys to disappear into that inky darkness.

Only Wise Owl slowed his pony and looked back, in time to see the great Chief stoop to enter his tipi, closing the flap behind him.

Wise Owl left to find his family. He ate a quick meal and returned to the tipi of the great Chief. Bear Chief beckoned him to his side.

"Do not be afraid of me, Wise Owl. I need your help tonight. It is about the infant you brought to me."

Wise Owl looked to the ground. "I will tell you what I can." He paused to gather his thoughts. "We were playing in the grasses after herding the ponies into their rope corral. I heard a mewing sound and we hunted to find it. We thought it was a baby mountain cat." He paused long enough to draw a deep breath. We found the bright cloth in the grass and I bent over to see it was a woman. She was dead. Again we heard the mewing sound. It was coming from under the woman. I jumped back, and Dances in the Rain caught me."

"And then what did you do?"

"I told Comes At Dawn to roll her over. He did. We saw the bundle. It mewed again."

Wise Owl clasped his hands as in prayer. "We caught three ponies and Comes At Dawn handed me the bundle. I knew you would know what to do."

What did you do with the dead woman?"

"We tried to put her on the horse but we were not strong enough." All of a sudden Wise Owl started to shake. "Wolves came. I saw three of them. Their eyes were glowing like an evil spirit. We left the woman to the wolves."

Bear Chief drew the young boy close to him. "You were brave, Wise Owl. You saved your brothers. You saved this infant. There was nothing to do for the woman. Go home. Sleep. I am proud of you."

Bear Chief reached into a small pouch strapped to his waist and pulled out a very small piece of the calico cloth. "This is for your medicine bundle." You were named by the shaman when you entered this earth and he chose well. You are brave and loyal to your chief."

Bear Chief smiled but the boy could not see his face. He coughed. "I have asked the Great Spirit to fade this day from you and your brothers' memory. It will be so. Flower Woman has named him Little Bear. He will grow up in my tipi. You will be his guide."

Wise Owl puffed himself up tall; filled with pride at being given such an honor. He doubled his right hand into a fist, raised it over his heart and struck himself on the chest twice. "I will take care of your family forever." Wise Owl looked off into the distance. Somehow he knew from this day forward his life had changed.

"The white men from Fort Shaw will come here. I do not want you to talk to anyone. You will go with Flower Woman and help hide this infant." Bear Chief released the boy. "Tell no one what you have told me tonight."

Wise Owl left on the well-worn path. "I made a vow tonight. I will find a good pony to pull the travois."

Flower Woman came out of the shadows. "I heard you give Wise Owl the assignment to guard me and Little Bear. I will follow him and see that he completes the mission." She paused only for a second. "After the people are gone we will celebrate our son and give him his name." She tenderly touched Bear Chief's cheek. "Then we will single out Wise Owl and give him a precious owl feather for his medicine bundle."

Bear Chief watched Wise Owl as he ran down the path to his tipi. "He's going to strut like a peacock."

"Are you worried he won't keep the secret?"

"I know our people; our secret is safe with him. We have many children in our camp from many tribes. Many babies are born after nine moons from the latest rendezvous that are the seed of many mountain men. Who knows what color their skin is under all that hair they refuse to cut or comb." He grabbed for a handful of Flower Woman's long black hair.

"Our only worry might be Many Moons. She is related to that disgraceful Crow. Curly speaks like a white man with a forked tongue after a barrel of fire water."

He walked to the tipi flap and beckoned for Flower Woman to join him inside where the chilly night air would not reach them.

"I will send a messenger with the demand that Many Moons and Looking Back and the children leave with you and Wise Owl. The Nation's people do not speak English. They do not trust Blue Coats and will avoid them. Our secret is safe."

Flower Woman happily lay down, snuggling into Bear Chief's warm robes. She held Little Bear near her heart and hummed the love song she had learned as a little girl. The Blackfoot song had lingered in the evening air the night Bear Chief showed he favored her. It was at a spring gathering of all Nations. *Everything was as it should be. I will thank the Great Spirit for this blessing of happiness and for Little Bear.*

━━◆━◆━◆━━

F LOWER WOMAN, EXHAUSTED from her birthing ordeal, lay sleeping on her side. She had pulled her legs into a fetal position. Her pad was laid out in the rear of the tipi. Some of the outside hides had been rolled up and tied to the poles to let in the night air. Bear Chief's heart saddened as he watched his woman who sat beside him and slept in his robes. Now she started rolling sideways. *She is dreaming that bad dream again. The Shaman did not take it away.*

Bear Chief needed to wake Flower Woman; talk to her about this baby he held in his arms.

Last night she had given birth, only to have the bad spirit sneak in and suck the breath from her stillborn infant; too fragile to fight for his life. Her mother, Many Moons, had called for the Medicine Man and the best drummer in their village. Neither was filled with enough power to chase away the bad spirit.

How will Flower Woman react when she sees this little one? Should I do it or should I have a runner take him to Fort Shaw, where the father might be waiting for some news?

Just then a lusty cry filled the tipi walls. Bear Chief had the choice taken from him as he looked at Flower Woman. She stared, wide-eyed at the baby. Bear Chief cradled him into Flower Woman's right arm. She did not speak. The baby felt her warmth, making sucking sounds. As if by magic, the newborn found her swollen breast, and milk poured from Flower Woman. She looked up at Bear Chief. The pent-up tears spilled from her eyes, down her cheeks. She reached to grab Bear Chief's hand. Laughter, manic in sound, came from her belly and out her mouth.

"What kind of cruel trick is this? Whose baby is this?" She saw the brown eyes, white skin and brown hair. "What have you done? This baby is a white-man's child."

Bear Chief dropped to a sitting position. He leaned forward and raised his hand to touch Flower Woman's cheek. "I don't have answers. I will send Eagle Feather to Fort Shaw. Why the baby is here? I don't know."

Flower Woman looked from the baby into Bear Chief's eyes. She saw his love for her and concern for this baby. "Maybe the Blackrobe who stayed in our village on his way up river was right when he talked about the white-man's God. Could it be *their* God who sent us this baby?" She shuddered as fear took over. We must hide him." Flower Woman turned her attention to the baby she cuddled next to her heart.

"Don't bring evil thoughts into our tipi. I'll find Eagle Feather tonight."

Bear Chief stood, took one more look at the infant, and then exited the open flap. *Flower Woman has already bonded with this baby. I will have a son to carry my name.* Bear Chief smiled.

The white man will mourn his dead wife. By now a search party would have recovered her body, or wild wolves have dragged her to their den. Bear Chief's worry was for the young boys who had come upon this grizzly sight. Blue coats will come to camp very soon. I must go to Eagle Feather tonight.

⸻ ◆ ◆ ◆ ⸻

3

B EAR CHIEF WALKED to the plain hide tipi of Eagle Feather. The tent flap was up and Eagle Feather stood in the entrance. He felt it in his heart that Bear Chief would come to visit him this night. He had not made a fire and the darkness hid him. He watched Bear Chief approach and he whistled to him.

Bear Chief nodded his head; together the men entered the dark tipi.

"As your Chief I am sending you on a mission. Listen to your Chief."

"Today Wise Owl and other boys found a dead white woman lying in a pool of her own blood. Next to her was a newborn, barely alive but able to whimper. The woman must have used a sharp rock to sever the cord, and then wrapped this tiny spirit in a ragged piece of calico cloth ripped from her dress. Wise Owl carried the bundle back to me."

Eagle Feather looked into his Chief's eyes. "What do you want from me?" He crossed his arms, covering his bare, muscled chest. He reached up to grab the eagle-claw neck-piece, given to him at birth. He never took it off. Tonight his spirit power felt heavy.

"You speak and understand the white-man's tongue. You are a warrior." Bear Chief breathed deeply. "You listen to the mountain men at rendezvous. You are a hunter. I need your many skills now." Bear Chief stretched out his arm to touch the eagle claw neck piece.

"Leave tonight. Go to Fort Shaw. Find soldiers and listen to them talk about this dead white woman and this infant. Do not let them know what you know. Be back in camp before tomorrow's sun sets."

Bear Chief did not wait for an answer. He turned and walked to the tipi flap. In one swift movement he slipped out into the darkness.

Eagle Feather followed him outside. "I will leave now." He handed Bear Chief a beautiful sacred eagle feather; one he kept near the tipi flap. About a year ago, he had made a vision quest inside an eagle trap on the mountain the white man called the Bird Tail. The great bird came to him and flew into the trap. Eagle Feather pulled the bird's tail feathers then released him back to fly free; to take his prayers beyond the sun to the Great Spirit.

Bear Chief raised his arms and turned his palms down hovering over Eagle Feather's long braids. "May the warrior spirits keep you safe."

4

EARLIER THAT MORNING Flower Woman had crept away from the tipi. She and her sister, Looking Back, had gone hunting for bushes where the berries were plump and the ground felt cool to their feet. With luck, they hoped to fill a basket with wild strawberries, rose hips, dandelions and other herb plants that grew in the meadows. Flower Woman made great medicine from the plant stems, leaves and flowers.

Looking Back motioned towards the river. "Let's spend some time at the river, soaking in cool waters, and rubbing crushed petals in our hair." Neither spoke much; it was too lovely a day to not just enjoy nature. Flower Woman was due to deliver her first baby. She had dreamed she was to become a mother to Bear Chief's son.

That night the pain in her belly came in unrelenting waves and she felt an evil spirit leaning over her. She thrashed and screamed but still the agony continued. Looking Back's silent tears fell from her eyes as she tried to help her little sister deliver the baby.

"Push little sister." She held a ladle of cool water to Flower Woman's lips. She rubbed oils on Flower Woman's belly. "One more *push*." She caught the still form and wrapped a rabbit's fur hide around the baby, tying the bundle with a leather string. The tipi resounded in silence. The older women who stood guard outside the tipi flap waited to hear the first cry that never filled the evening air. Looking Back opened the flap. She motioned for her mother, Many Moons to enter.

Many Moons shoved her way past the other women and stepped into the red tent. She was angry. In her hand she carried a beaded medicine bag that she had finished only two nights before. She used special beads traded at the Bent's Fort to design a bear into the pattern. Many Moons tossed the bag onto Flower Woman's empty womb.

"How did this happen? The Great Spirit planted Bear Chief's seed in you. You have disgraced our Chief. He will kick you out of his bed, his tipi. You will live alone. None of your family will speak to you as if they do not see you walk by." She dropped her gray-haired head to her chest. Looking Back stood beside Flower Woman and held her hand during the horrible tirade coming from their mother. The evil spirit had gripped this older woman with feelings of shame and disappointment. Not for her daughter, but for her own status in the tribe. That would not happen now that she was not the grandmother to the great chief's son.

"I go to Bear Chief." Many Moons left the tipi and the women behind her. The bright yellow beaded moon shapes threaded through the tops of her moccasins would light her path to Bear Chief's tipi.

Flower Woman's heart smashed into shards. How could it keep beating? What will Bear Chief do to punish her? There would always be sorrow and she would never forget the birth pangs.

Bear Chief had been waiting patiently to hear the good news of his now having a son. When he heard footsteps coming up his path he hurried to open the tent flap. Many Moons stood before him. She pushed her way into his tipi and with haste told him there was no child this night. That Flower Woman was too weak. She showed no sympathy for her daughter or for his loss.

"What have you done with the still born?"

"Looking Back wrapped him in rabbit fur. Why do you care?"

"Leave this tipi. Never enter here again. You are a cruel old woman. I must go to the tent and rescue Flower Woman."

Many Moons stomped outside. There was nothing but evil for all of them this night. She turned back only once. "You know men cannot go into the red tent. That is sacred for women. Stay away. Evil Spirits will attach to you."

Bear Chief pushed her aside and ran to the birthing tent. "Where is Flower Woman?" He looked around the room. "Where is my son?"

Looking Back took him by his arm, and together they went to Flower Woman.

Looking Back unwrapped the bundle. There lay the most beautiful newborn, so still as if sleeping. Bear Chief picked him up out of the fur wrap. He held him to his chest. He kissed his head. He blessed his body. He handed the baby back to Flower Woman. Looking Back, Flower Woman and Bear Chief locked arms to make a sacred circle of three. Bear Chief prayed and sent the evil spirits away.

Flower Woman rose from her pallet and as one they moved down the path to Bear Chief's tipi. Looking Back tended to her little sister, making a hot broth of herbs for her to sip and return strength to her exhausted body.

She tried to thank Looking Back.

"Shh. Not now. You rest. Bear Chief is here. Many Moons is wrong. He will not kick you out of his tipi. We will honor your baby with good spirits in the morning. We go together to the sacred burying grounds and find a special place."

Flower Woman, her eyes heavy with sleep, lay back on her pallet.

EAGLE FEATHER RODE bareback clutching the animal's full mane for balance during the dark of night. They arrived at the fort fence where Eagle Feather had turned his horse loose. "Stay here." He knew the horse would wait for his return. He jumped the stone fence and disappeared through an open window into the storehouse. He looked on every shelf, wanting to find a shirt and pair of pants that would fit him. The Quarter Master's shelves were almost empty of uniforms meant for the enlisted men. He found what he needed and quickly changed into the regulation uniform: blue coat, pants, jacket, yellow bandana, and a pair of hard leather cavalry boots. He wiggled his toes. *How can a man wear these? My feet are not free. I must try to walk like a white man.* He stuffed his soft leather moccasins made from moose hide inside the waist band of the bright blue pants. *I cannot leave any signs that I have been here.*

He swung the eagle claw neckpiece around to hang down between his shoulder blades. He spotted the only floppy, wide-brimmed Hardee hat lying on the shelf. The hat sported a gold flying eagle brass-plated adornment pinned on the right side. Gold rope braid completed the decoration. Eagle Feather ran his fingers over the eagle pin and saw it as a good sign that he was being protected. He coiled his long braids onto the top of his head and covered his hair with the hat and tied the leather thongs under his chin.

Cautiously he opened the door, poked his head out to look left and right, and quickly stepped outside. The clothes felt too tight and uncomfortable; he stretched his arms over his head. *Best way to hide out is to stay in plain sight.*

By the light of dawn Eagle Feather confidently strolled around the back side of the supply building. A few dogs barked; not enough to alert the guards of any wrong doing. He found a four-legged wooden chair tipped over in the sand. *Ump! It was probably tossed out by a loser at the white man's game of cards.* He dragged the beat-up chair to the porch and sat himself in it. The front legs of the chair tipped high when he leaned back to stretch his legs to rest on top of the porch railing. Many soldiers, headed for the cook tents, walked past him; he felt invisible. *My spirit guide covered me from the not-quite-awake soldiers wanting a cup of strong coffee.*

Eagle Feather pulled the hat brim forward to shadow his hairless face, pretending to sleep. His arms rested on his chest, covering up the buttoned shirt underneath the yellow scarf. His right hand remained ready to grab the concealed knife he stored next to his beating heart. Another long knife felt secure strapped by leather strips to his right calf above the ankle.

Sgt. Sullivan walked briskly around the Commander's office opening the window panes allowing fresh air into the already stifling room. The prisoners had been brought up from the stockade, shackled and cuffed to a piece of pipe. They stood outside, some shaking beyond belief from fear, others shed uncontrolled tears. Two of them wet themselves when they heard their names being called.

Through half-closed eyes Eagle Feather watched the sorry soldiers come in line up the path to the office door. *They look so young. What offenses; what punishment is their fate?*

"Guard! Bring in the first prisoner."

The line swayed as the guard unlocked the chain and prodded the offender through the open door. The guard hit him between the shoulder blades with the end of a Billie club and the young soldier stood ram-rod straight. He waited for the officer to speak.

"What is your crime?"

"Sir! I left my post at the River's Crossing and stranded travelers who wanted to cross on the ferry." He looked to the floor. "I was tired and in my defense, sir, it had been a very long day. We sighted a line of Chippewa Indians on the top of the ridge, heading north. They had travois, dogs, and children. It looked like the leader was a chief."

"All the more reason you should not have left your post. Why wasn't this information revealed to me?" The prisoner stayed silent. "Thirty days in the jail at White Sulphur Springs." Bang! Down fell the gavel as it struck hard on the wooden block.

The guard grabbed the offender by his arm and tossed him towards the open door.

"To the wagon with ye, lad."

"Next!"

Eagle Feather sat still, waiting for the right prisoner to come before this officer. He had five more stories to listen to; one of these five would have what he needed to hear.

Some of the offences were trivial: fighting with other soldiers, cheating at marbles and card games. These men were sent back to the stockade for a cooling off period.

One soldier admitted he drank too much rot-gut whiskey and failed to shut the main gate. Escaping cavalry horses galloped through the opening. Eagle Feather had to cover his mouth to hide his smile. *Our braves would have stolen the horses, shutting the gate when they left.*

The Ute Tribe taking up land in Utah country had been spotted earlier that week on the high line headed north. It would have been an easy break-in for them to swoop through the poorly constructed fort while the soldiers slept in canvas tents. Children, young women and able-bodied men were their targets. It made no difference if they were white people, or from one of the many Native American Indian tribes roaming the plains. These abducted persons swiftly found themselves in Mexico working as slaves for the rich hacienda owners, toiling in all kinds of weather, for years picking crops, planting seed, cutting hay until they dropped dead.

Indian children made good workers. They were paid with food and a blanket. A dormitory held cots that they shared, each child having that space for eight hours each day. The Mexican government looked the other way. There would be war between Texas and Mexico soon enough.

The officer banged the gavel. He looked at the private with contempt. "Private, do you realize what you have done?" He did not wait for an answer. "White Sulphur Springs stockade, twenty-one days." The officer scribbled something on a form with his pencil and lifted a heavy metal stamp that he pressed on to the form; making his mark. "Solitary confinement and no visitors."

The wagon driver entered the office and grabbed the offender by the back of his shirt and tossed him outside. "To the wagon with ye, lad."

The last prisoner fell through the open door. He lay on the hard floor, afraid to look up.

"Guard. Is this the last of the prisoners for today?"

The guard saluted. "Yes, sir!"

"Then shut the door. I want you to leave him here. Tell Sgt. Sullivan he has his load for today. He can take them back to the stockade for tonight and deliver them to the jail in the morning."

The General rubbed his forehead. The heat was bringing on a headache. The guard prodded the young man until he stood up. "I'll be outside, sir."

Eagle Feather leaned further back in his chair, almost resting his head against the open window. This would be the man Bear Chief sent him to find. *My eagle spirit, stay sharp, with eyes that see everything and ears to hear. Protect me.*

⸻ ❖ ❖ ❖ ⸻

6

BEAR CHIEF WALKED his morning circle but his mind and heart was not active. His thoughts were centered on Eagle Feather. He chanted so softly even the birds in the nearby trees did not hear him.

Spirit of Eagle Feather guide your charge today. Keep him sharp and alert. Protect him from the dangers he is in. Keep him safe from the hundreds of soldiers patrolling the camp. Put him in the right places to help us uncover this mystery.

He heard the baby cry. In just a few hours of being with Flower Woman the little guy showed his stamina. Bear Chief smiled. He had made a decision. Flower Woman will keep the child. The secret will stay in the tribe and the elders will not be told. The very thought of a fatal decision from them to kill the baby left him cold and nauseous. Flower Woman had begged him all through the long night that he let her keep this infant from the spirits. She named him Little Bear.

Last night as she reached into the large reed basket that held the swaddling clothes, diapers, gifts meant for her baby, her hand pulled out the empty beaded medicine bag. The firelight flickered and Flower Woman saw the careful design. A little brown bear walked across the top of the bag. *I must show this to Bear Chief. It is a sign from the Great Spirit. This infant is to be our child.*

All day the couple kept Eagle Feather in their thoughts. He would be returning soon. Flower Woman cut a curl of the baby's hair. She laid it out on the rug. Then she put the calico cloth between her teeth and ripped off a strip. This would go into the medicine bag. She broke off a piece of sage, dried rose hips and other dried berries. A small round cut from a deer antler, about the size of a silver coin, was dropped into the bag. Each item she picked up and examined carefully, knowing the bundle would not be opened again until Little Bear earned an honor and a ceremony took place. With love she wrote out on a small piece of tree bark how Little Bear came into their lives. Since she only knew the oral Blackfoot language, she drew stick figures, so in future years someone would discover their bundles and know about the miracle of Little Bear's life.

Little Bear started to fuss. He was hungry; she was ready for him to nurse at her breast. With a quick pull of the leather strings, she closed the bag, patting it carefully. She hung it on the pole where Bear Chief and Flower Woman's bundles entwined.

Bear Chief watched her doing this sacred ritual for a newborn Blackfoot baby. He nodded his head in agreement with Flower Woman. She faced him, took his hands and smiled.

Where is Eagle Feather? Will we be able to keep the baby a secret? Bear Chief, one who rarely showed affection, pulled Flower Woman to his chest. He held her close as she calmed her fussy Little Bear. Her milk overflowed with love like clear spring water falling from a mountain waterfall.

As promised, Looking Back entered the tipi to help Flower Woman. She was taken by surprise when she saw how fast Flower Woman had started to recover from her terrible ordeal only a few hours ago. Then she heard the meowing sounds. "What is happening?"

Flower Woman lifted the blanket. Looking Back was shocked.

"Where did you get this baby? I don't understand." Looking Back reached down and picked up the brown eyed, brown-haired, white skin baby.

"The Great Spirit brought him to us. His name is Little Bear." Flower Woman pulled Looking Back close to her. "Please don't tell anyone about this. Bear Chief and I will go to the sacred burial grounds now. I need you to keep watch over our newborn. We will explain everything when we return."

She and Bear Chief made their way to the red tent. The woman who had guarded their little one stood up on very shaky legs. Her knees popped when she straightened them. Bear Chief thanked her for her loyalty to her tribal traditions and for staying all night in the red tent. Then Flower Woman and Bear Chief made the lonely walk to the burial grounds. Bear Chief carried a shovel. He would open Mother Earth and together they would give over their child to her. The hole swallowed up the little bundle of fur. Bear Chief dropped the dirt back into the hole. A small pinion tree marked the spot should they ever pass this way again.

May the Great Spirit direct your path with a bright light. Bear Chief chanted until he could not speak. Flower Woman spilled tears until she could wail no more. Bear Chief held Flower Woman close to his chest. He looked over the top of her head, out into the prairie grass and surprised, pointed his outstretched finger. "Look!"

Flower Woman turned to see a magnificent Grizzly bear walking through the tall grass, sunlight shining brightly, parting his long hairs. The bear stopped, turned to look at them, grunted and continued into the bright sun. He moved to stand near the pinion tree. Then, to Bear Chief's surprise, the Grizzly bear dropped to the ground to keep watch over their Little Bear.

"SOLDIER! STAND WHEN you are spoken to."

Eagle Feather slowly turned his head toward the voice. He dropped his feet to the porch floorboards and stood.

The Captain saluted and Eagle Feather clumsily returned the motion.

"Why are you lounging here? Move along with you; get food before it is tossed to the dogs and the pigs and chickens."

"Yes, Sir!" Eagle Feather picked up his battered chair as if to move it aside.

The officer continued down the planks and walked into the make shift kitchen. The wind had picked up and was blowing fine sand everywhere. Eagle Feather noticed that the men who wore the Kepi hat were ducking their heads. Some had tied their yellow bandana around their face, squinting their eyes as they scurried across the field from their tents to the kitchen. When they approached an officer, however, they stopped and saluted the man; waited until he had passed them by.

Eagle Feather returned to his spot beneath the open window. I hope I have not missed too much of the talk going on between the Commander and the prisoner.

"Recite your name, birth date, rank, and where you enlisted." The Commander impatiently waited for the young prisoner to speak.

He is a private from Pennsylvania. How'd he get attached to this unit?

"Sit." The Commander pointed to a wood chair in front of his desk. The shaking soldier sat. The officer remained standing and started to pace the office space. He held a small whip in his right hand and occasionally struck the desk edge. Old marks lined up on the edge from previous abuse.

"Where were you six nights ago?"

Shivering as if cold the private tried to keep his body still. "I was in Bent's Fort sent there to pick up a woman and her belongings. She came up river, and needed transport to this fort, sir."

"Did you do as instructed?"

"Yes, sir."

"Did you know her name?"

"No, sir."

"Talk to her about coming to this territory?"

"Yes, sir. She sat next to me on the wagon box."

"Did you deliver her to the fort?"

No, sir."

"Why not?"

Eagle Feather's attention steadied on the voices and he did not see the officer return.

"Soldier! Why are you still here? I told you to move on." The harsh tone startled Eagle Feather and he jumped to his feet.

"I wanted to stay in the shade, sir." Eagle Feather saluted.

"Why are you dressed in blue? You should be fed and to the mud yard by now."

He paused, giving Eagle Feather a closer look. He took note of the skin color; decided he might be of African descent. Hundreds of soldiers who fought in the black unit under General Shaw during the War Between the States, or the Civil War as northerners tagged it, came out west. They had no place to call home and following General Shaw showed honor and respect. It also meant their future could be in this new land.

"Button your shirt when not working. I don't want to see you lazing about when we need mud bricks. We need at least 2000 bricks from you today."

"Yes, sir." Eagle Feather lowered his head to look at the buttons. His bandana had turned enough to uncover the collar. He straightened the material and picked up the chair.

Humph! White men build everything with corners. They do not look to nature. We make everything in circles: Tents, fire-pits, cooking pots, tree trunks; even dogs circle their sleeping ground before they lay down. The wind blows leaves and grasses in circles, clouds are circles in the Big Sky. We do not make sharp corners to trap us. Circles have no beginning and no end.

The officer walked on by and Eagle Feather waited only a few minutes to make sure it was safe for him to return to the window.

Anxious to hear the conversation still happening inside the office, Eagle Feather carried his chair to the back side of the square mud brick building. He found another open window with a large pinion tree growing near it.

Ah. This good spot. Eagle Feather hid behind the tree, pulling his feet under the chair legs to make him as small as he could.

Off in the distance, Eagle Feather noticed a line of leafed-out cottonwood trees. Men were filling wagon beds with sawed off tree trunks. A group of men worked two-handled saws to cut lengths for firewood and kindling. A sawmill buzzed making long boards for building supports. Other soldiers had the job of filling barrels with water needed for making the mud bricks. The river flowed fast. A trench was being dug out from the fort to the river's edge.

Eagle Feather longed for a drink to sooth his parched throat. His hat, now soaked in sweat around the brim, helped cool his head. His feet were swelling in the leather boots. Eagle Feather needed food but that would have to wait. He pressed close to the window, hoping the officer would not walk to the window to look outside. The voices continued, harder to hear from this location.

"Did you bring the woman to the fort?"

"No, Sir." The private closed his eyes tight as if to shut out a memory.

"Why not?" Down came the whip hitting the chair the soldier sat in.

"I...I..."

"Out with it."

"I left her on the road, Sir. I saw a group of Indians off in the distance and I thought I should get to the fort as quickly as I could. When she asked for a stop-break I helped her off the wagon seat....

near a tree." The private looked at the officer with pleading eyes. "Sir. She was with child…she would hold me back…Sir?"

"You COWARD!" Down came the whip; this time striking the prisoner on the shoulder. He felt the blow and the sting but did not cry out.

"A good soldier would have stayed with her until the very end, even at the cost of his life. The Indians are not at war with us. We have a peace agreement with all the plains tribes." He turned and leaned on his desk.

"That woman was my *wife*!" The officer was screaming now. The guard opened the door and looked inside the room.

"Stay out!" The officer kicked the door closed.

"I put you in the stockade to keep you from deserting. I wanted to kill you. I want the whole story and then I will decide your fate."

"She told me to go on; she would be fine until I returned with a doctor. She said she was about to have her baby." The prisoner started to cry. "I didn't know what to do, so I left. We have a doctor and hospital help; that's what I went for."

"You drove away from my wife, about to give birth to my child?" The officer slumped into his chair. "I didn't know any of this." He took in long gulps of air and tried to steady himself before he could continue. With some composure the officer spoke so low the private could not hear him.

"She wanted to be with me and homestead out here when my replacement comes." He buried his face in his hands. "Oh! God. Why? Why did this coward have to be the one who went for my wife?" When he finally looked up, anguish mixed with streams of tears trickled in rivulets down his cheeks and into his beard.

"Continue."

"I told the gate guard what had happened and he sent troops and a wagon to bring her here. They could not find her; no body, no trail. The guard did find a torn square of cloth and one of her shoes hidden in the grass near the tree where I left her."

"What about the infant?"

"They found no sign of an infant; blood stained the grass."

"My God, my God…" The officer composed himself and his thoughts. *She could have been found by those Indians and they are taking care of her and the baby. I'll never stop waiting for her. My son is alive, I feel it.*

"You are a despicable human being. Killing you is not a punishment. I'll see to it that you *die* but not by a bullet." He shouted to the guard to come in to witness the sentence.

"Sgt. Sullivan take heed. "Send troops to Bear Chief's camp. Take a translator. Ask if any woman with a newborn came into his camp. Have the men look into tipis."

The officer stumbled back to his desk. He stared into the young man's tormented face.

"You! COWARD! Stand up. Be a man for once in your sad life."

Eagle Feather memorized this information. He had what he needed to now leave Fort Shaw. Bear Chief would know what to do with the newborn baby that Flower Woman wanted for her own.

The prisoner stood on shaking legs.

"Your sentence is as follows." He pointed to Sgt. Sullivan. "This guard and another man of his choice will take you back to the place where you left my wife. You will be stripped naked and your boots taken from you. A gag will be stuffed down your throat. Twenty lashes across your bare back will draw blood. Mosquitoes will sting you and birds pick at your wounds. Buzzards will circle overhead waiting for you to die. The guard will chain your hands behind your back and he will clasp irons on your legs." The Commander shut his eyes. "May God forgive us."

Sgt. Sullivan saluted the officer. "Your order will be carried out within the hour, Sir."

Eagle Feather memorized this information. He had what he needed to know and he stood up, spilling the chair back into the dirt. Bear Chief would know what to do with the newborn that Flower Woman wanted for her own. He looked around. *I must be alert and wait for the right moment to escape these men.* Just then a huge eagle flew up from the river carrying a fish in its beak. As it neared Eagle Feather it swooped low and dropped the fish. Eagle Feather devoured the fish. *Thank you eagle spirit for my food.*

Eagle Feather heard the black stallion whinny and saw him paw at the ground. The animal whinnied again as if to say 'come here,' we have to leave now. Eagle Feather, walking in the too tight boots, headed slowly in that direction where the horse waited. No one noticed him. The men were running in the opposite direction, past him to peer into the wagon.

The prisoner, naked and bound, was slumped into the wagon bed.

"Where's he goin'? Nobody spoke up. "Anybody know his sentence for what he did?"

"I heard he killed the Commander's wife." Another voice shouted out from the gathered crowd.

"Looks to me like they going' to kill him. They'll save his uniform for the next sucker to join up out here."

Sgt. Sullivan climbed into the box and picked up the reins. He gave a quick slap to the horses' read ends. The men jumped back, clearing a path. Some stayed and watched until the wagon passed on through the makeshift repaired gate.

Sgt. Sullivan motioned to the guard to jump aboard. A cloud of dust flew up in the wind and that was the last anyone at the fort saw of the young private from Pennsylvania who dreamed of fighting Indians in the West.

The black stallion appeared at the edge of the dust swirl. This was the chance Eagle Feather had been waiting for. He made a dash through the open gate, left unattended long enough for him to rush to the stallion. The horse, so eager to return to camp, almost left Eagle Feather standing in the dust. One powerful leap sent strength through Eagle Feather's legs; horse and man became as if one. No one paid any attention to the fleeing horse and rider.

8

T HE DRUMS ALONG the trail to Bear Chief's encampment grew louder the closer the tribes arrived. Excitement filled the air. This gathering held opportunities with honor ceremonies planned; family members meeting after a long stretch of separation. Those arriving first had already set up their camps along the river and children splashed in the water.

Everything looked normal. Bear Chief greeted each guest in the Blackfoot traditions by offering food, blankets, prayers; asking what was needed to make the next five days pleasant. If anyone thought it strange that Flower Woman was not at his side, no one commented.

Eagle Feather rode directly to Bear Chief's tipi and told him what he had heard. Bear Chief nodded occasionally but did not interrupt. Flower Woman held Little Bear close to her heart. What would Bear Chief do now that he knew the white man will come from the fort?

"Thank you for your speed in returning to me." He handed Eagle Feather a bowl filled with a red liquid. "Drink this tea that Flower Woman prepared from her herbs. Get food and rest Eagle Feather.

When the soldiers come I will need you to translate." Bear Chief laid his hand on Eagle Feather's forehead. "The sweat house is waiting for you." Eagle Feather gulped the blessed tea, and then slipped out of the tipi. He had released the stallion with the other horses and Eagle Feather watched the beautiful animal roll on his back, stand up and shake off the weariness. *I'll do the same for my body.*

9

T HE MEN, HELD in the stockade, nervously awaited the return of the last prisoner. Why hadn't he been brought back to the group? Did he get sent to White Sulphur to the jail there? Time seemed to stand still until they saw the guard coming towards them.

"Well, buckos, ye'll not be seein' that room-mate ever again." The guard sat down on a barrel full of water, crossing his right leg over his left knee. "His sentence is almost as horrible as the crime he committed."

The men gathered close to the door. "What you mean? Tell us straight out."

"I mean he has been sentenced to death out on that desolate flat land. I took him to the exact spot where he dropped off the woman." He rubbed his neck and face. "Sure did hate to leave him, but orders is orders, you know?"

Each man looked at another and none spoke. *Leave him to die?*

"The woman was comin' here to live with her husband." None other than the company commander hisself." The guard, a fellow corporal who had served under Gen. Thomas Francis Meagher, stood up. "Hardest thing I ever done. May God have mercy on all of us."

"What did you do to the guy, shoot him?"

"Worse than that. I was ordered to shackle him in chains, bind his hands behind his back, strip him naked, even take his shoes and socks, and turn him loose to starve or be drug off by wolves." The guard shut his eyes tight as if to blot out the scene. "He won't last a day in this heat. The whip lashes cut deep and blood covered his back when I stopped. That brings flies."

The sky darkened as evening descended on Ft. Shaw. The prisoners were not thinking of food when they heard the bugle sound *last call for supper*. "It's now or never if you want to eat," said the corporal. "Here comes your new guard." The guards exchanged salutes. The new man on guard-duty paid little attention to the prisoners. The men, now recovered from the news, waited until they were sure the guard had walked to the back side of the make-shift building. The walls were solid, windowless. As if they were one, the idea to pilfer through the missing man's belongings hidden under his cot struck. Whatever they grabbed they claimed as their own. One of the highlights for *findings* was a gold hinged locket showing a beautiful young lady staring back at them. "Lookee here! What I got." The man standing next to him liked what he saw. *After he's asleep I'll get that for my own.*

A packet of letters tied with a blue ribbon was claimed right off. "Do you think the gal in the photo wrote these letters? I don't know how to read so's they's no good to me. Anybody want em?"

"I do," said an outside voice. The commander had been watching them all along, hiding under the cover of darkness. "You…You who has the letters, come forward." He waited only a few seconds. "Guard, open the lock and find those letters."

"Yes, sir!"

The command was obeyed; the young private from Arkansas handed over the letters.

"I'm going to my office, soldier." He again exchanged a salute, turned and walked back up the path to his office. *These letters must be destroyed.*

The first letter was missing a stamp. It was addressed to his parents in Pennsylvania. The soldier was probably waiting to send it back home first chance he could get postage. Benton's Fort sometimes had stamps in their make-shift post office. He started to read the message written in a flowing hand. The writer obviously was educated in schooling and came from a family high up in society.

He wrote:

Dear Mother and Father,

It takes a while for mail to reach me, and again a while when I answer all of your questions about the Army life here on the high plains of Montana Territory. I am stationed at Fort Shaw for now. I hope this ends in three months. I will be mustered out as a private if The Peace Treaty between the Blackfoot Indians and us is kept intact.

You will not recognize me as the rebellious son who ran from all you offered me with a life of riches. I wear leather buckskin clothes with fringe on the sleeves. My hair is so long I keep it braided and hidden under my Kepi when in uniform.

Taking orders is hard; the food is terrible, except for the bread. I Surely do miss Cook. She is the best.

The weather is burning hot now and absolutely unbearable in the winter.

I have been assigned to the commander of this post and I drive a supply wagon to Benton's Fort. It is about a half a day away.

We are digging a long ditch for water flow as there is no water at the fort yet. It is not safe; full of salts.

Also, I am on the mud-brick-making team. I have to load water from the River into barrels and drag them behind horses about a mile. There we mix the water and dirt and pour it into wood forms where it sets up very fast in this heat. We are ordered to make 2,000 of these mud bricks per person, per day, per soldier. We have crews working on building quarters for the officers and their wives; a building for supplies and places for a kitchen. I am developing muscles in my arms and legs. We sleep in tents on cots, eat in tents, and have a limited yard to walk in for exercise.

We do go hunting for wild meat, like deer. We raise chickens, dairy cows; Have a great bakery, and fat pigs.

I am sorry for my behavior last year. Believe me, I am maturing in so many ways. I pray this letter reaches you soon. I'm through with Army life forever.

Your son,
James

The commander put the letter down on his desk top and reached for a cloth to wipe the sweat that had seeped from under his hairline. *My God, what am I going to do? I must get control of myself and decide what is best for the Fort. This letter could cause an investigation from Washington, D. C.* Too tired from this emotional day, he put his head down on his desktop and wept. He slept the night right there in his hard office chair.

T HE KNOCK ON the office door startled the commander. He woke up confused by his surroundings.

"Who's there and what do you want?"

"Sir! It is morning. You need to get breakfast."

Slowly the officer stood from his hard wooden chair. "Come in, Corporal. Thank you for locating me." He walked out the door into the fresh morning air and headed for the latrine. A square of tin hung on the wall. The commander gazed at his bloodshot eyes. *I've aged 10 years over night.* He ran his fingers through his beard and hair; brushed down his jacket and stepped out of the box. *I need a strong cup of coffee.* He made his way to the kitchen tent, lured by bacon smells floating in the wind.

He spotted Sgt. Sullivan and went to his side. "Sir! Please sit down. I have news concerning yesterday." He paused for a minute, looking at his commander. "Your orders for the prisoner were complete. Today we will hunt for his body and bury him in the soldier's cemetery."

"Yes. We cannot give him a ceremony, since he died a coward. But he should be buried. I will write his family today; the next assigned wagon driver will mail it from Benton's Fort."

"Yes, Sir!"

Another secret, another lie. This has to be put to rest. I'll not send the letter the soldier wrote full of army life and future plans. I'll write a personal note saying he deserted and we have no idea where he is, probably on the run to California. I'll burn the letters and his belongings today. If his body is found he'll be put to rest here at the Fort. He will have a wood cross marking his place, since he was a Christian, but no information is to be carved on it. I'll give orders to Sgt. Sullivan later today. The official Army papers I'll mark as a deserter and put them in the files. I cannot read any more of this man's dreams and words written by the one who loved him. I'll never forget his cowardly ways towards my wife, and the child I knew nothing about.

"Well done, soldier." He reached for the bacon and egg platter and took a helping on to his tin plate. A stack of flapjacks drenched in real butter and maple syrup filled his empty stomach. Coffee never tasted better to him and he continued to eat in silence.

The wagon wheels screeched and the harness jangled as the horse pulled past the window. Sgt. Sullivan and another guard, riding shotgun, saluted the guard at the gate.

"Think he's alive?

"Naw." The man shook his head.

"Well, I hope so. If we don't find a body we can be sure he was drug off by wolves. No chance he could walk to help. The Indians haven't been spotted by our scouts for several days. Even so, they'd have brought the man to the Fort for help. There's no homesteaders around there. Keep a sharp eye out for him as the grasses are tall and could hide him from our sight."

The man shuddered. Army life lost its splendor at that moment. "I'm gettin' out as soon as I can. I heeard Virginia City is lookin' for men to find gold."

Sgt. Sullivan laughed out loud. "You might be one of the lucky buckos, but don't think too far ahead, son. Life changes every time you blink an eye."

The corporal looked off into the distance, lost in his own thoughts, wanting to get this assignment behind him; afraid to think of what they were going to find.

"There! Over there! Stop the wagon." He jumped from the box and ran to the mangled, gnawed, bruised remains.

"I found him, Sir!" He stood back in the grass and waited for Sgt.

Sullivan to pull up alongside of him. "Let's load up that sorry sight. It will be dark before we get back to the Fort. We can spare the other soldiers and do the buryin' before we report back to the commander."

B EAR CHIEF WAS busy. He welcomed all the chiefs from the Plains tribes, and by the third day over 10,000 had gathered for the rendezvous. Each year members of different tribes, except the Crows, set up tipis along the Missouri River. Friends met old friends and made new ones. Children played with tribal cousins, and the mountain men *hallooed* to every one making a grand entrance. The women giggled and put their hands over their mouths as they watched these bearded white men straggle in with half-wolf dogs, long rifles, back packs, a few with horses; some had wagons full of trinkets to use as trade for favors. The women soon would be flocking to these wagons anxious to be first to see the precious items. One special treat they all wanted were sewing thread and needles with big eyes for beading on their looms made from tree branches.

Drummers with handmade drums showed off their skills at making the drum; many claiming theirs' the best because they used soft, pliable horse belly hide stretched tightly with animal leather thongs knotted around the perfectly cut oak trees. The sound of the beat vibrated soulfully. When eight men gathered in a circle the drum beat became a contest. Who could keep up with the changing pace? Each tribe had a favorite drum beat and when it was played, many chanted the tune to the song. Most of the songs had no words, but the tunes and beat would echo throughout the camp. Twenty-four hours a day drummers gathered to play together. Dancers strutted in bright feather costumes and women dressed in fancy leather, beaded in bright beads traded at the last rendezvous. The young women left their hair long, black as ink. They decorated their head with flowers, beads, ribbon strips to try and catch the attention of the braves who strutted like peacocks around the fire. A happy, playful attitude permeated the grounds.

Even the women from Bear Chief's camp were excited to see so many other women. They brought food from their tipis to make one long line of food for everyone to eat when they wanted to. Time for meals was forgotten. Children raced to the food line every time new items, like grasshopper cookies or fry bread was set out for the taking. Working in groups made it easier for the women. No one complained if the younger girls did not help out. They remembered their own youth and how they gathered to dance and sing and find husbands from other tribes.

Flower Woman and Wise Owl were hidden away but they knew what was happening in camp. Looking Back had her hands full keeping the younger children out of sight and away from the camp. She, too, longed to join in the fun. It had been several seasons now since her husband had been killed in a skirmish between the soldiers and a few Blackfoot men who were hunting meat for their cooking pots. Bear Chief cared for Looking Back and her children. Flower Woman had her place with him as his wife and they all accepted the arrangement and were content with it.

Flower Woman stood in a grove of Cottonwood trees and listened to the drums. She was thinking about Wise Owl. *He is being very quiet today. I wonder what he is planning to do*? I must talk with him. Just then she heard a sharp cry from Little Bear.

When she ran to the tipi she saw Wise Owl holding Little Bear. He was grinning; looked so pleased with himself. "We can go back to the camp now, Flower Woman. See what I have done?"

He held out the baby's hand, palm side up. Flower Woman gasped. "Is he hurt? What happened to make him bleed? Then she noticed Wise Owl had a piece of cloth wrapped around his hand and blood trickled beneath his crude attempt at wrapping the wound. A hunting knife dripped blood that Wise Owl had laid on the table.

"Little Bear is now my brother. Forever we will be joined in our blood. He is mine to teach to be a warrior and we will be friends now and in the hereafter." Wise Owl handed Little Bear to Flower Woman. "You will be his mother and Bear Chief his father. That is the way of our tribe. My blood now flows in his blood. See? He no longer cries as if hurt. He smiles and is happy. He is one of us. He will live in Bear Chief's tipi. He will be his first son with many more to come."

Wise Owl, what can I say? You are very clever. You have a bond brother as well as a blood brother. He is no longer a white man's child according to our traditions." Tears welled up in Flower Woman's eyes. "Thank you child of Looking Back, my nephew." She rubbed his head and said a blessing to the Great Spirit. "This child is my child. It was meant to be that you found him and brought him to Bear Chief." She smiled. "We no longer have to keep a secret. Then she scolded the boy. "Don't ever try this again without talking to me. There are herbs you should have used to clean off the wound. I hope he and you won't be left with a scar."

Flower Woman shouted for her sister. "Looking Back, where are you? Come here and bring Many Moons and the children. We are going back to our tipis and we are going to dance and be happy once again."

Looking Back hurried to Flower Woman. "What has happened? Are you ill?"

"Of course not. Wise Owl, your very clever son, cut himself and then cut Little Bear. He rubbed his young, red blood into Little Bear's palm and arm. He made a vow to be his brother and teach him our way. They are now blood brothers." She held up Little Bear's arm. Looking Back was speechless.

Flower Woman grabbed Looking Back and they danced in a circle around Wise Owl.

"Someday very soon, Wise Owl, you will be a right-hand helper to Bear Chief." She turned to stare at Many Moons. The younger women had forgotten she was with them.

"Many Moons you must be silent about this child. Do you understand? Bear Chief will put you out of the tribe and leave on a trail for you to find another people willing to take you in; a useless old lady who cannot keep tribal secrets. I will see to it myself if you do not listen to your Chief."

Many Moons turned her back on her daughters. "I'll not tell anyone, but I'll never love that white man's child." She started to pack, anxious to go to her own tipi and be a part of the only world she knew.

The camp had quieted down now that it was late at night. The food keepers were clanking pans, whispering, laughing, and very tired as they finished cleaning up the food left on the long boards used as tables. The long, straight lodge poles from the travois served as braces for the rows of boards holding the plates of food. The women of each lodge kept track of their handmade basket trays and carried them back to their tipis. They would bring them back in the morning full of breads, berries, boiled eggs, and wild meat, whatever they chose to share with others. This lessoned the work load for Bear Chief's women.

Bear Chief lay on his robes, longing for Flower Woman to be at his side. He knew she was safe and able to care for herself wherever they were camped. She would not build any fires as smoke would give her away. He thought he heard scratching at the back of his tipi.

"Bear Chief, it is Flower Woman. I want to come in."

Bear Chief grinned. "Then enter through the tipi flap. I welcome you and Little Bear. Why are you back here in the dark tipi creeping? Has something happened?"

Flower Woman tossed her head back and laughed. She looked happy and this puzzled him. "Look at Little Bear's hand. See the bandage? Wise Owl cut himself and then he cut Little Bear They are blood brothers forever." She stopped talking as Bear Chief held up the tiny hand.

"I've already scolded him. But I also blessed him for his actions today." She paused.

"Wise Owl is indeed well named. He will become a right-hand helper to you very soon."

"What about Many Moons?"

"I told her to listen to her chief. She said she will keep our secret. I told her you would kick her out with no water or food by the side of a trail. No one would want an old, useless woman who cannot keep sacred the tribes traditions and secrets."

Bear Chief laughed. "Would you really do that?"

"Yes. For you and for me and for Little Bear? Yes. I would do that."

Just then Little Bear gave a loud hungry cry and Flower Woman took him to her breast. She smiled as he found her milk. *Thank you Great Spirit who knows how to make everything right.*

T HE TWO BLACKROBES joined the encampment on the second day. Their journey on the steam boat from St. Louis to Benton's Fort had been long. Forty days of fighting mosquitoes along the Missouri River route, scarcely eating, praying and teaching about Jesus Christ and a religion called Christianity, kept them awake nights. By candle light they wrote in their journals recording every event of the day. Loss of sleep almost took its toll. When they arrived at Bent's Fort the noise and disruption disturbed them most of all.

"Can this really be our calling to be here in this god-forsaken place? There is no church, only one white woman at the mercantile; no place for us to rest." The older priest, a Jesuit and follower of Father Pierre DeSmet complained constantly.

"Father why can't you be more positive; trust that God has sent us on this path?" The newly ordained young man felt excited about this mission adventure. He was eager to find the great Bear Chief's camp. "Here we are able to save thousands of souls and bring the truth to these people. How fulfilling can that be? I pray every day for our health and our words to be kept strong."

The black robes stood out as they walked to the entrance of Bent's Fort. "We will find a room for us to rest." He stopped to read the handmade sign hanging on the open gate. "This is where we are to meet the man who sent for us."

Bent's wife looked up, startled to see the men in the black robes with hoods covering their heads. "Oh! Come in…Do come right inside. Have a drink of water, or something stronger if you want it. I think we have wine for special occasions in the back." She was all flustered. "How can I help you?"

"Thank you. Yes, we both need water." The younger priest gulped down the ladle filled with water in a wood bucket. "We are in need of a place to stay. I did not notice a hotel. Can you direct us to one?"

"A hotel. Well, now…that is not possible. However, I have an extra room you can share at our house." She went to the open door and pointed the way to a white stucco small house just up the road from the mercantile. "Make your way up there. My husband is at home taking a lunch break. He will show you to the room." She smiled. "Welcome to Bent's Fort."

"Thank you, Ma'am. God bless you for your kindness." The younger man grabbed his companion by the arm. "We must be on our way. Father Michael is tired and in need of rest."

"I'm in need of a decent cup of coffee." The man grumbled as he walked out the door.

"Now, father, you must rest and be sociable. We have a mission that will begin in the morning. I'll get information, and find a wagon and horse to buy that will take us to this Bear Chief's camp. You'll be teaching, praying and baptizing the Blackfoot Nation by tomorrow evening."

The men continued their walk up the dusty, rutted road, jumping out of the way of loose cattle being herded by men on horseback. "Isn't this wonderful? I have read about the Wild West but I never thought I would be a part of it." He turned to help the older priest across the street. "Just think of it. We will be in our community's history books."

The rusty hinges squeaked on the iron gate as the priests passed through. A waist-high picket fence, once painted white, attached to both sides of the gate. "Humph. That's certainly not heaven's gate." Father Michael grumbled.

"Look at that huge river boat pulling in across the road. Listen… hear that fog horn announcing its arrival?" Father Jerome stood facing the river long enough to store the scene into his memory bank. "What a wonderful gift our superior abbot has given us, don't you agree?"

"He sent us to answer the request of his friend who is the Bishop in Helena, Montana. He didn't want to come all this way himself. You just watch. In a few years we'll be down here at this town waiting for another steam boat to come in with that old goat on it wanting to see what we have accomplished."

Father Jerome was shocked at this sudden outburst. "Father Michael are you ill"? He waited for a reply but none came. Bent, seeing the two Blackrobes at his gate, had opened the front door to greet the men with abandon.

"Finally. You have arrived. Now we will get some civilization in this part of the country. The Indians are peaceful now, but we fear there will be another uprising soon. A renegade band likes burning down farmer's barns. Sorry to say this but anything the white man does on their land is destroyed; churches can't keep ministers and without a minister there is not much for a congregation."

He looked at the younger priest. "If we get some religion into those redskins maybe they will adjust to the new way of doing things." He shrugged.

"Come inside. I have a good back-east coffee ready for you and some cookies my wife made yesterday. We have been looking forward to your arrival almost every day this past couple of weeks. When you didn't come off the boats we assumed the worst. We need what you and your God brings to all of us." He took note of the priests' small leather strap bags. "Is that all you carried with you?"

"We have cargo at the dock. After we find a horse and wagon, we'll pick it up and be on our way to Bear Chief's camp."

The interior of the house was very small, but ample for the merchant and his wife. Bent took three coffee cups from the one shelf for dishes that hung near the kitchen table and chairs. He filled them with the strong black coffee. The aroma immediately brought a smile to Father Michael. He sat in the yellow wood chair and reached for a cookie. The fancy china plate was piled high with delicious sugar cookies usually made at Christmas time. The priests sat quietly listening to Bent talk about the town.

"Not much here as you've already noticed. But just wait. This river landing is the first town for the boats and they are working all hours of the day and night bringing supplies which I sell to the homesteaders." He pulled back the frilly white curtain so they could see outside to the street. "My wife doesn't *like* living here. She is lonely for her *real* life. Buffalo Gals who follow the riffraff don't make for her kind of friends." He shrugged his shoulders and sighed. "She'll be wantin' to go back to the states before winter sets and she gets trapped here by the weather.

Bent dropped the curtain back and wrapped his fingers around his coffee cup. "Hell, there are days I want to go with her. Probably will when I can find someone to work the mercantile. The fur trade is strong here and keeps me plenty busy." He looked at Father Jerome.

"Tell me, what are your plans?"

"Our plan is to build a mission somewhere near Fort Shaw, Montana Territory. We need government financial help as well as money from the parishioners and the Diocese of Helena. We want to open a school; teach English, mathematics, and writing for starters. Of course our main purpose is to tell these people about our Heavenly Father God. Surely there are gifted Blackfoot people who will listen and take advantage of having their children learning the new world way of living, don't you agree?" Father Jerome paused. Bent's eyebrows closed in upon the bridge of his nose.

"First, we have to get you some transportation. It is way too far for you to walk."

"I need to purchase a horse and wagon at a decent price." Father Jerome wrung his hands. "We have very little money as we are to be like Jesus and search daily for our bread."

"Well, I can help you with the horse and wagon at a cheap price since you are not particular about what the horse looks like, or if the wagon has two wheels or four. I have a two-wheeled cart that will hold your meager belongings, at least for now." Bent stood up. "You rest a bit. We can discuss the price after you see what I have to sell." Bent showed the men the guest bedroom. He pointed to the latrine outside in the back yard.

Father Michel kicked off his sandals to give his swollen toes a chance to breathe and lay back on the small, but comfortable bed. Father Jerome fell to his knees and gave a prayer of thanksgiving that the older man seemed was way too long. *Time for praying after we rest. Lord, what have we signed on for? Will this be where I will spend the rest of my years? I will try to accept this new lot in my life, but you are going to have to send me signs from the Holy spirit…*Father Michael was fast asleep before he could finish his thoughts.

Father Jerome heard the snoring coming from the other side of the bed. My, my. This is going to be a thorn in my side if Father Michael can't see the joy in our assignment. If he continues to show signs of great distress and maybe an illness, then I'll be forced to write to our superior and ask for advice.

Jerome lay on his side of the bed but did not sleep. He waited to hear the jangle of horse harness announcing Bent's return. "Dear Lord, this generous man wrote asking for us to come to this territory. Now we are here and in need. Can you give him word to donate the horse and cart? Thank you Lord for keeping us safe in your care. Amen.

Without another thought, Father Jerome sank deeply into the feather bed and did not fight the comfort. Sleep overtook him long before Bent returned with the horse, cart and their baggage he'd claimed from the dock.

13

S UNSHINE WOKE THE two priests from a much needed and deep sleep. Father Jerome smelled the tantalizing aroma of breakfast being made. Coffee, ham, potatoes and homemade bread greeted him when he walked out the bedroom door.

He had left Father Michael still in bed, but saw that he was stirring. Bent had things cooking in the kitchen and there was no sign of his wife. She had left to open the mercantile.

"Ah. You are finally awake. I started rattling pans a bit ago." He motioned to Father Jerome. "Come and sit. Coffee is ready for a bit of sugar and cream if you like it a little less strong."

Jerome sat and said a prayer over the food being cooked for him by this generous man.

"Do you like working among the savages?" He asked.

"Yes and no. The men trap animals and bring their hides to me; trade for supplies. The women want beads, needles, seeds, cloth. It is a very busy season and their hides are in excellent condition. Beaver is still a top seller for me so I buy them all, and then ship them down river to a dealer in St. Louis. Beaver hats are popular in England, so these beaver hides from here possibly make it across the ocean to become a stove top hat for some English royal."

"Hmm. I see." Father Jerome bit into the bread. "Your wife makes good bread."

Bent laughed. "I'm the cook in the family. She helps out with the mercantile and works long hours working with the customers. So since

I like to eat, I have learned to make a few meals." He pointed a long handled two-pronged fork at Father Jerome's plate. "That there food is my favorite to make." Both men laughed and drank more coffee. A scuffling sound stopped them. It was Father Michael, awake and up and ready for the day. The older priest came into the kitchen and went straight to the coffee pot.

"Well, Father Michael, I see you are up and dressed. Come have a good hearty breakfast. You might not eat again until late this evening." Bent pulled out the ladder-back kitchen chair and the priest gratefully sat down.

"Harrumph. I need my coffee. Then we can talk about supplies and be on our way."

I see his disposition isn't much better this morning, but that will change when we get to our destination and start building our mission. Please Lord; let me be correct in thinking this positive way. Help me to understand the drastic change in Father Michael's attitude.

It struck him like a thunderbolt. Father Michael is afraid of the Indians; of this mission. Lord, protect us as we wander into the unknown. Maybe I should be just a bit more cautious myself?

Bent cleared the table of the used dishes but left the coffee cups in place. "I've got the horse and cart outside in the corral." He walked towards the door. "Let's go have a look-see."

"That cart is just what we need." Father Jerome inspected all sides of the run-down cart. The wheels were made from cottonwood tree circles. "We can handle it easily, and it will take us where we need to be. It will haul things. How much?"

"Well, now, not too fast. Let's see the horse next." Bent gave a sharp whistle and a sway-back worn out workhorse came to the pole fence line. "Have some sugar, old boy." Bent pulled a hard white sugar crystal out of his jacket pocket. The horse carefully grabbed the lump. "Do either of you know anything about horses? What they eat, need, keep their hooves clean; stuff like that?" The three men looked at each other, and then turned to look again at the horse. "You need a wise old horse like this one, who by the way, answers to any name you want to call him as long as you whistle first." Again the three men looked at each other. "One of you does know how to whistle, don't you?" Father Jerome laughed out loud. Father Michael harrumphed.

"How much? For the outfit?"

"Me and the wife talked it over last night. We sent for you to come here to help get this community up and running. So, we are going to donate the horse, cart, all the necessary harness you will need to get you where you want to go." He grinned. "One of your faithful tossed in a gunny-sack full of oats to keep this here nag happy."

"Thank you Bent. I prayed that you would be generous to us, and that prayer has been answered." The young priest made the sign of the cross and blessed the cart and animal.

"Now, let's go to the mercantile and get you some supplies. The wife drew up a map for you to get to Bear Chief's camp. She has it with her as she wants to visit a bit before you take off into the unknown."

Father Jerome noticed their suitcases stacked in the rear of the cart. "Why, you stopped at the docks for our baggage. That will save us time today. I hope to find the Indian camp before dark."

"You'll hear the drums way before you get to camp. There is a big pow-wow going on this week and thousands of natives are arriving from all over the West."

The men returned inside the house, packed up their simple belongings and headed for the yard where Bent was harnessing the old horse.

He paused for a moment and looked at the two priests. "Wear your black robes in safety today. If you stay a few days, watch and learn different tribal customs, pick up some words from the mountain men." This time he stared at the sky and seemed a little wistful. "I wish I could take you there and join in the festivities myself. But the wife, well, she won't mix up like that. Trading with them is about as far as she goes." He motioned to the two men. "Hop in."

Father Michael sat on the hard piece of wood that passed for a bench. "Harrumph."

Father Jerome took the reins in his left hand and tried to make the old horse move. Bent laughed until he cried real tears at the sight of those two good-hearted priests full of ideas of saving the natives. *Little do they know what lies ahead.*

A hearty greeting met them at the mercantile. Word had spread that the Blackrobes had arrived. The community was very happy to finally meet them. Bent's wife came forward and pulled Father Jerome into the circle that filled the main part of the building.

"Here is a map of the territory that I made up. It is not drawn to scale, but it does mark trails and locations." She handed the rolled up paper to the younger priest. It had a red ribbon tied firmly around it. Father Jerome accepted the paper. *That ribbon just might come in handy if we need a peace offering.* Several women came forward bearing gifts: Blankets, bread, berries, jams, garden seeds and one handed Father Michael a lilac bush wrapped in burlap and dirt. One grandmotherly type woman handed over her gift. It was a pouch full of wet flour. "This is sourdough. You will never go hungry if you keep this mix alive. You can make pancakes, but be sure to save back a handful each time. It grows on its own and when you can, add some flour to make it thicker. Keep it wet." She stepped back into the circle.

Men brought crude, handmade tools, a shovel and wooden barrel bucket, hammer and lantern with a wick and kerosene for the lantern. These were precious gifts and useful. The leader of sorts, asked for a blessing.

"Father Jerome made a sign of the cross over the group. He pulled out a white handkerchief and blew his nose. "We thank you all from the bottom of our hearts. We will remember you in our daily Mass and in our prayers until we meet again. Now...we must be on our way." He smiled as he looked at each person in the circle. "If any of you are looking for work, please come visit us. We will be at Fort Shaw for the time being."

One old trapper raised his hand over his head. "You'll hear them drums and you'll know you are gettin' near. There's a big pow-wow goin' on. Thousands of injuns will be there. You'll see some on the same trail as you. Let them pass you by if possible. If you hear gunshots it's 'cause an Injun found a wild deer to bring meat to their fire." He stepped back into the circle wearing a big smile. "I'll be seein' you before long at the camp." He sized up the two priests. "Pick up a few words from us mountain men if you can. That'll show them you care about them." This time he stopped talking and stared up at the ceiling.

Father Michael's knees had started shaking from the delay. He didn't like the hard bench for a seat. "Enough talk. We must be on our way."

Father Jerome stepped inside the cart and grabbed up the reins in his left hand. He tried to make the old horse move forward, but that wasn't happening. Bent took off his hat and walked up to the horse. One slap on the behind was all it took to get things started on down the trail.

14

E{VENING BREEZES MADE} travel easier for the Blackrobes as they pushed the horse and cart onward to find Bear Chief's encampment. Thoughts swirled through the older man's head. *Are we welcome here among these savages? Have any of them heard of our Lord God? Or have they any idea who Jesus was? Those drums are getting more insistent with each mile.* "Ouch! Another rock on the trail to make my tailbone sore."

I'll try to drive better, Father. It is just that this horse has one speed and I don't think he sees too well anymore." Father Jerome lifted the reins and gave the horse a little slap on his behind. "The drums are rather stimulating, don't you think?"

"Stimulating? I find them irritating."

All of a sudden the horse stopped in his tracks. Off to the side, Jerome stared into the face of the first Native American he had ever seen. The man had black painted stripes from his forehead to his neck; white circles surrounded his eyes and feathers stuck up in his braided hairpiece. The Indian was just as startled to see the two Blackrobes sitting in a cart.

"How?" said Father Jerome as he raised his right hand in greeting.

The Indian sat on his horse and blinked. He hit his mount in the ribs and in a flash headed for the encampment, shouting some kind of a chant, a warning maybe?

"Now maybe you will be more careful and listen to me, said Father Michael. "That man will send a war party and kill us before night fall."

Dances In The Rain, galloped straight to Bear Chief who was standing on a makeshift stage giving a speech to the gathered family. "They are here, Bear Chief. I saw them. Two Blackrobes will be here very soon." He hopped off his horse and went onto the stage with Bear Chief. "The need help finding the camp entrance. We must help them. Follow me."

Immediately a happy chaos spread throughout the group. Men riding bareback met at the edge of the camp. "We are ready. We will bring them to Bear Chief." About 20 warriors left to greet the priests.

The squeaking wheels rose higher than the beating drums. Father Michael saw them coming. "Oh Lord in Heaven, help us."

When the Indian with the black stripes reached the cart, he slid off his horse and grabbed the harness on the old horse. "Welcome. My English is poor. I will say no more."

The Indians closed ranks around the plug horse and cart. They escorted the priests into the encampment. Bear Chief, Flower Woman, Little Bear, Looking Back and Wise Owl stood tall wanting to see these white men in strange black garb.

Some of the villagers pointed fingers into the horse's belly and laughed at the boney ribs. Father Jerome waved and smiled and made several attempts at trying to make the sign of the cross in a blessing. He felt excited and happy. *This is where I am to do God's work; by God that is what I will do.* He did not look at Father Michael. *I want to remember this greeting forever.*

"Bear Chief, with Eagle Feather at his side to translate, raised his right hand as if to make a blessing over the two men. "May the Great Spirit who brought you here keep you safe."

Wise Owl tugged at Flower Woman's skirt. "May I take the horse to the corral? The horse needs water and food." He smiled. "The cart needs to be emptied; their things placed in the tipi that was set up yesterday for their visit."

"Yes Wise Owl. Take care of these men. Show them our way of welcoming them into our tribe." Flower Woman gave him a little shove towards the men. She pointed her finger at Father Jerome and attempted to say his name in English. Eagle Feather stood by her side and translated her message into English. "Go with Wise Owl. He helped set up the tipi for you. He will bring you back here for a feast in celebration." Little Bear squirmed, not liking to be disturbed while he slept in loving arms.

Bear Chief waited until the cart had been moved and the warriors had taken their horses back to graze. He had very important news that must be told this night. The whole village needed to hear what was going to happen to them.

"Listen to your Chief." He stared out at the gathered ones. "My scout, Wolf With Eyes That See, brings bad news. The Bluecoats are going to come here to our village before the next full moon. They will force us to pack everything and move to a place in the backbone country, closer to Canada. That place is called a *Reservation* by the Government. We have no say. They want this land for homesteaders who farm and turn over the soil to plant hay and corn."

A cry that started as a murmur from the Indians in the front of the group, soon turned into wailing and screaming from the women. "We cannot let them do this to us."

Eagle Feather tried to quiet them. "Listen to your Chief. He will know what is best for us to do." Many warriors are saying *fight* them, but there are too many bluecoats for us to do that."

"This is happening because of Curly showing the soldier with yellow hair where to find us," said an older warrior. "He was promised good things, like ponies and land for guiding the Yellow Hair soldier and his troops. Eagle Feather did not have to translate for Bear Chief.

"We must not break the treaty; at least not now." Bear Chief called for all the sub-chiefs to meet him in the big tipi. They needed a plan to move everyone safely. Some of the visitors would stay in camp since they had already moved to come to this rendezvous. Others, the old, the weak, women and children, would need strong arms to help take down their tipis when the time came. Bear Chief, head held high, with Flower Woman at his side, made his way to the meeting tipi. Men wearing dance clothes and clay masks who had prepared for a night of unbridled lust and the white man's rot-gut, followed as if in a parade. They had one focus; sit at the circle inside the big tipi.

The Blackrobes, now forgotten, looked about them in dismay. Father Jerome was confused. "This can't be true. We were sent here to start a mission. The Government would not have allowed us to do so if the Indians are to be pushed away. The Glacier country is very far away." Father Michael's lips quivered as he silently said a prayer for their safety. "Please, Lord, I am too old for this. Don't let them take me captive or torture me like they have done to so many other priests."

Father Jerome was astonished as he heard the frightful words from his companion. Well, now I have the answers I prayed for last night. We two are certainly going to keep our "Great Spirit" busy with this assignment of building a mission.

The two priests hurried to stand outside the large tipi. They listened to what sounded to them like gibberish, so they kept moving to the tipi. Father Jerome took the arm of his companion. "We will leave in the morning, very early, so don't unpack anything. We must find Fort Shaw and ask for advice." He did not light a fire inside the tipi. Two large buffalo hides were spread out on the ground. He pointed to the hides.

"Father, this will have to serve as our beds tonight. Aren't you happy we had the comforts of the feather bed at Bent's home?"

Father Michael paused for only a second. He only knew he was tired, hungry and frightened to be in this Indian camp where he couldn't understand the language.

"I'll wrap up in this scratchy, hairy robe, but I won't shut my eyes. You can if you want since you'll be driving tomorrow. If you hear me scream, run away."

The night air, now carrying a cold wind into the tipi, swirled around in circles surrounding the two men who were unaccustomed to any kind of outdoor living. It looked like a long, hungry night ahead.

"Yes, Father, I'll be listening for your alarm." Father Jerome wrapped up in his robe. He turned on his side, shut his eyes and pretended to sleep. *Good Lord, you have brought us this far, help us to understand both worlds. Amen.*

The drums continued to beat soft and slow, gently lulling the priests into a merciful sleep.

Bear Chief waited until all the sub-chiefs were seated around the tipi walls. He would enter and sit cross-legged in the center of the circle near the back side of the tipi. All would face the burning fire lit by Flower Woman who had backed her way out of the tipi, not wanting to see her shadow from the fire's bright flame. Dancing shadows on the walls would cause enough concern to those who looked for 'signs.'

She found Looking Back and sat next to her. "Where is Wise Owl? We need to find him and send him for more wood for our fire-pit." Their purpose was to keep food ready while the men talked. Looking Back stood and looked over the young men who had gathered outside; wanting to hear what was being said. She spotted Wise Owl and called him to her side.

"What is it mother?" He was anxious to get back to his hearing spot at the tipi edge.

"We need wood."

Bear Chief lighted his long ceremonial pipe, took a puff, and then looked to the West. With each direction, West, East, North and South he beseeched a different spiritual power. He acknowledged Mother Earth; hitting the ground at his feet with the pipe. The sixth recognition was to the sun. Bear Chief pointed the pipe to the sky. He thanked the Great Spirit for his life and held the pipe straight upward. His final prayer was one of thanksgiving. "Oh, Great Spirit, thank you for the powers of the universe, both physical and spiritual."

Slowly he passed the pipe to Eagle Feather. Eagle Feather passed it to the man next to him and this tradition continued until the pipe came back to Bear Chief; the pipe ceremony complete. While in the hands of Eagle Feather, he paused to examine the pipe. He had made it many seasons ago, hollowing the insides by fire and smoke to push beetles to eat their way out the stem. This took a long time and patience on his part. It had been many moons since he'd seen the sacred pipe used only for special ceremonies when help from the Great Spirit was sought.

He had carved design on the exterior of the pipe. Tonight he was looking for cracks and found none. The work was high quality. Special feathers and black, red, orange and white ribbons adorned the area around the mouth piece.

"Listen to your Chief. The government thinks they are helping our people by pushing us into the backbone country. They named this land as our *Reservation*." Several of the men snickered at the word. Another shouted, "You mean they want to put us into a pen like an animal." A chorus of words echoed off the tipi walls. "We are not children without souls who must be babied so we don't hurt ourselves playing with fire-sticks. Even the river is bad for us to fish in." The shouts continued to grow more intense. "We are Mother Nature's children."

Bear Chief looked across the circle of sub-chiefs and stared at one rabble-rouser. "We cannot fight them; even though we are strong, they are many. We will not break the Peace Treaty. To do so would bring only death to our Village. Do not think of warring with the Bluecoats. We will move…"

Grunts of disagreement reached the women's ears. "This is not good for us. We will die of shame if not from hunger." Looking Back shut her eyes tight. She did not want Wise Owl to see how her eyes flashed with anger and hatred toward the white man.

Bear Chief stood; his arms making an 'X' across his vest.

"Listen to your Chief. I will prepare soon for a vision quest. My Spirit Guide, the bear, will send me signs. All of you guide your brothers to seek wisdom and have patience." With that statement Bear Chief shrugged. This time he reached for the short pipe and took a long draw from it before passing it to Eagle Feather. When all had smoked, Bear Chief raised his hands and poured out a blessing on all who would accept it.

He noticed the sullen face of one warrior, Dances In The Rain. I will tell Eagle Feather to keep watch over him and see if he holds secret society meetings while I am gone. Turning around to face the flap, he walked outside into the now dark sky. Hum…No moon, no stars, and no wind. Not good sign.

Flower Woman ran to his side. "Please, Bear Chief, I want to ride with you. "Looking Back will care for Little Bear."

Before dawn came Father Jerome had Father Michael seated in the cart. The old horse, not ready to leave the tall grass covered with morning dew, wouldn't come to the gate. Father Jerome had the harness spread out; all he needed was the horse. He whistled but it did no good.

"Can't you go grab his mane or something?" Father Michael needed coffee. He tried whistling, growing more frustrated with the passing moments. "Say a prayer that the old nag thinks it's Bent and he has sugar." This time the horse responded and came to the fence gate. He nickered for the sugar. Father Jerome grabbed on to the mane and slid the head harness over the old nag's ears. He patiently worked his way through the many steps to hitch horse and cart.

"At last we are on our way. We're going to wake up the whole village, but that can't be helped. We must find Fort Shaw."

With the first turn of the wheel the screeching sounds began. Wise Owl, sleeping under the stars with a robe for warmth, jumped to his feet. It was his job to watch over the priests. He ran outside in time to see the cart leave camp. *I'm in trouble. I was supposed to see they ate food and then guide them to the trail leading to Fort Shaw. Too late now.* He shrugged his shoulders; looked left and right; saw no one. *I'm going back to sleep.*

When they reached the top of the bluff Father Jerome halted the horse. He dug around in the cart until he found a jar of jam and a loaf of sour dough bread that had been gifted to them at Bent's Fort. He tore chunks of bread smearing the jam over the bread with his finger. He handed one chunk to Father Michael. Little did they know Indians from the secret society were following them. They would make sure the Blackrobes made it safely to Fort Shaw.

Father Jerome unrolled the hand-drawn map. The distance startled him. The trip would take longer than he originally thought. He would push the old horse, allowing for short breaks but keep on the move towards the safety of the fort.

The horse, however, had other plans. It needed water and grass. During the heated part of the afternoon it finally gave out and stopped right in the middle of the trail. Nothing said or done could get the old horse to take another step while hooked to that cart. The sun beat down on the priests dressed in black.

"We have to stay with them. They'll never make it on their own," signed the lead Indian.

The other men sat their horses and covered their mouths to stifle their laughter at how helpless was the white man when in nature. The band stayed hidden in the grove of bushes and trees. It provided cover, shade and grass for their mounts. The river flowed fast at that bend in the oxbow, carrying any sounds away that might reveal their hidden horses

Father Jerome had unhitched the old horse from the cart but did not turn him loose. He made a loop in the long rope handmade by a cowboy who was a day-hand at a ranch outside of Bent's Fort. He slipped the loop over the horse's head. It was loose enough to allow the animal freedom to move around, nibbling grass. The other end he tied to the cart. *I hope this idea works. I don't know how far we'd have to walk if it doesn't.*

The lead Indian watched the priest, surprised at how clever the man turned out to be.

"Best we picket right here. I'll take the bucket down to the river and carry water for 'Old Faithful'. He can find enough grass to nibble on right here." He also picked up the canteens. "Some good clean cool water will taste like French wine."

"Father Michael, please try to find a way to secure this blanket over our heads to provide some shade, and stay near the cart. This is not the time to wander off looking for a bush to hide behind. If you need to relieve yourself, do it on the trail behind us." He also took note that the high wind was pushing in dark cumulous clouds that looked like they were full of rain.

"I'll dig out some more of that bread and jam. Maybe there is dried jerky packed in that gunny-sack?" Father Michael looked around him and realized how alone they were in this vast wilderness. He tried not to show worry in his eyes. "Hurry back. Yell if you need me."

The Indians watched with amusement. They would remain hidden so as not to embarrass the white men, but at the first sign of distress they would show themselves. Their well-trained horses remained still, not once nickering to the old horse or giving away their hiding place.

The Indians realized how naïve these Blackrobes were and that this would be a good first lesson for them living in the Wild West.

15

THE BUFFALO ROBES kept the two priests warm throughout the cold night after the harsh wind settled down. Father Jerome kept watch as he tried to be comfortable on the wood bench in the cart. Father Michael chattered prayers and took up most of the bench, making sure his feet and hands were covered and warm from the blanket.

"Did you hear that?"

"Hear what?"

"It sounded like a coyote howling right over there in those trees." Father Michael pointed to the grove of cottonwoods that grew along the edge of the Missouri River. Little did he know those trees were sheltering the Blackfoot men who were playing tricks while keeping watch over the two Blackrobes.

"I didn't hear anything except the wind blowing hard making those tree leaves flap." Father Jerome lied; he *had* heard sounds all through the night. He was afraid to step out of the cart for fear a rattlesnake would be curled up by the rear wheel. He certainly wasn't going to tell the older man about his apprehension; at least not now.

Bent had warned him about snakes, coyotes, wolves, mountain cats, bears and anything else that could harm them. The priests did not have a weapon for defense, even though Bent had offered a pistol and bullets.

"God will send angels to protect us," he had told Bent who shrugged his shoulders and looked to the ground.

"Suit yourselves."

Father Jerome's face lit up while he was thinking of their supplies.

"We do have some cooking knives should we need help at the mission."

At the crack of dawn the two men were moving on down the trail. Every turn of the squeaky wheel brought the cart closer to the fort. They shared the last of the loaf of bread and drank water.

When the sun was high overhead the priests saw signs of human life.

"Well, would you look ahead, Father? See. There is wood smoke in the air, and I see soldiers moving about in that field. They are digging a ditch." Father Jerome gave a slap of the reins. "Come on old boy, we are almost to the land of milk and honey. Hooray!"

Father Michael stared at the early morning sight. When he did speak it was a thank you prayer. "Dear Lord, I am thanking you in advance for a hot cup of coffee."

The Blackfoot guards veered right and galloped back the way they had come. "Bear Chief will wonder if *we* got lost and he'll send a search party out for *us*." When they were sure they were out of the soldiers sight, they yelled a few whoops and raced their beautiful horses back to Bear Chief's encampment.

"I'm ready for a good breakfast." As if on cue the horses took off racing each other for the first position. Would the Alpha win?

The cart screeched its way to the gate, surprising the guard on duty.

"Well, well. What a sight for sore eyes. Welcome to Fort Shaw." He motioned for them to pass on through. "Go straight ahead to that building on your right. That is the officer's headquarters. We have been expecting you." He waved the cart and horse on through to the fort side of the stacked stone fence. *Thank God you didn't arrive five days ago.*

A warm welcome greeted them by a Corporal who was standing outside the officer's office. "Before we do anything let's get you some coffee and a good meal. The General is busy at the moment assigning camp orders for the day to the different crews who are working at building this fort."

They followed the smells to the kitchen mess tent; were greeted like royalty, and for the first time Father Michael smiled, bowed, talked, ate way too much, and laughed at little jokes the soldiers tossed their way. At last, I am safe. This is the first meal we've eaten in several days. We'll be given a tent to set up our belongings for as long as we need to stay here. The homesteaders and soldiers will help with the building of our church and mission house.

"Isn't that right Father? Father? Have you gone someplace in your thoughts?"

"Oh! Why yes, I have. I'm anxious to settle in and have a rest." He smiled. "The Lord has seen us safely here; we will have the first Mass this coming Sunday and I expect many soldiers attending that memorable service. The sun will shine down on our work." Father Michael raised his hand blessing the men who had gathered around him.

Sunday came and so did the rain. Lightning and thunder, torrents of wind, and hail the size of golf balls fell relentlessly. Only a few soldiers, soaked to the skin, remained outside until the hail started hitting their bared heads. A dismayed and discouraged Blackrobe peaked outside the large four-sided tent. *Welcome to this historic Mass.* He put away the chalice and plate, thankful he had not started saying the prayers.

16

*B*EAR *C*HIEF *LOOKED* *and felt tired. How many winters have I lived as the Chief of this Village? I've lost count. Today I feel like a very old man. It is time to have a new chief, but who? The younger warriors want to lead our people. They are too hot blooded and eager to fight. They have nothing to base decisions on past history and traditions. There is danger for their future. Soldiers are building more forts. They will never let us live in peace again; on our own land and with our traditions.*

Bear Chief sighed as he stood up and walked to his prayer tree. I'll hang some pretty colored ribbon strips onto the branches and hope the spirits see them. Answers might come to me after I hang the ribbons.

Flower Woman has given me many sons and daughters. She follows the Christian Great Spirit. Father Jerome poured his holy water over her head and she called out the name of Jesus. She is what is called a Christian. Many of our younger children are also followers of the white man's religion. Even though she wants me to join her, I cannot do so. I am too old to believe anything but what I learned from my father; he taught me well about our spirit guides.

I am happy that my family has learned to read the white man's words and can speak their tongue; their future will demand that of them. Bear Chief remained lost in his thoughts. He sat under his decorated tree and lit his pipe. He stared up at the beautiful snow-covered granite peaks that seemed to pierce through the blue sky.

Many seasons had passed since the great exodus of the Blackfoot

Nation from Bent's Fort to the Backbone country. Most of the village had accepted being pushed north and west near the country the white man named Glacier Park. Settling into a new location didn't affect the youngsters. It was the old people who knew another way of life who complained to him. They did not want to live behind a fence, eat handout spoiled meat and sleep in square houses. Bear Chief understood their anger. It was demeaning and wrong to be treated like little children not able to fend for themselves. He felt pulled in many directions.

Many hours occupied his time meeting with government agents. Few of his attempts for compromise were listened to; most shelved for yet another meeting.

Difficult changes were forced upon the village, but life kept pace with the rest of the world. Bear Chief's scouts and runners kept him well informed as to what was taking place, not only in their area, but throughout the vast West.

He was told the Blackfoot Nation would be cut even smaller when they were pushed even farther into the mountains, and in another direction towards the Canadian border. Whenever another wagon master lead his paid customers from the east into their Valley Bear Chief watched and wondered where they would declare their property. Sometimes the wagons stretched for miles as if there was no end to the white man's exodus. The Dakota land had been split in two, now called South Dakota and North Dakota; still one of the greatest land masses in one location for settlers.

The government kept building more forts and reservations for the Indian tribes who had no choice but to watch their homeland being taken over. To watch Mother Earth be turned by a plow, crops planted in straight rows flourishing under the hot summer sun, water flowing through a river that ran backward to the north was painful. Dams stretched across canyon walls, covered their sacred burial grounds. All of these changes tore at Bear Chief's heart. Homesteads haphazardly built in the corner of their allotted land were surrounded by barbed-wire fences, and white man laws prohibiting the Indians from hunting and fishing angered many of the tribes. How did the government expect them to survive?

Bear Chief heard rustling as Flower Woman sat next to him. "Where are you Bear Chief? I've been calling your name and you are not hearing me." She reached out to him and grabbed his long braid. "Your hair is as gray as mine. We're getting old. Have you been thinking about days gone by?"

"Yes. I am full of questions. I have been asking the Great Spirit for answers, but they do not come." Bear Chief shook his shoulders and arms.

"Do you like living here, Flower Woman?"

She did not answer right away. "I don't like the way we are being treated by the white man. Why can't we live our traditions and just let us be happy?" She took a deep breath.

"The last couple of winter seasons have been very difficult and hard on my bones." She looked up at Bear Chief. "The wind blows cold and snow covers us for too many moons." She smiled. "I like being wherever you are; where our children, my family, live."

After a pause she continued her conversation with the greatest chief in Blackfoot history. "You have directed our tribe through so many changes that other chiefs did not have to face; did not know about, or suspect that our traditions would be challenged like they are now."

Bear Chief tried to stand up. His hips and legs did not move like they used to. Flower Woman grabbed his hand and pulled him forward, keeping a tight hold on him to steady him until he could walk beside her without fear of falling. "I'll ask Eagle Feather to make you a fancy walking stick."

"The renegade bands are roaming around Fort Shaw. My runner was here last night. We smoked a pipe and then he told me the farmers are worried. They are sending their female children to the mission for safety." He steadied his moccasins firmly on the gravel path.

"The farmers are carrying firearms with them at all times. Barns and houses are targets and at night the Indians ride in and set fire to them. Hay-stacks are burned; horses and cattle disappear by morning." Bear Chief stopped and looked at Flower Woman.

"I can't control them. They will not listen. This destruction is not the answer. All it does is bringing more soldiers in to the fort; more white men come as fighters and guards for the farm people. Distance is no longer a good thing for the Indian. Homesteaders are being given acres of our land by the government." Bear Chief dropped his hands towards the ground. "We are helpless to try to stop any of this. Certainly both sides can see who has the best weapons and more men to fight us. We cannot win."

He pulled a letter from his leather fringed shirtfront. I had Eagle Feather read me this paper. It is from the Government. We cannot have any sun-dances, pow-wows or a rendezvous because it is disturbing to the white man's way of living." Bear Chief shook the letter into the air. "This is supposed to be our land. We signed treaties years ago saying we could live our old ways." Anger slowly changed the color of Bear Chief's face. "I sometimes want to join the renegades when these things happen that are unfair to us."

Flower Woman remained very still. She could add nothing to his thoughts. They stood together and watched the sun drop behind Chief Mountain. Darkness descended earlier each evening, or so it seemed to her. Soon winter would send them into a kind of semi-hibernation. She broke the silence. "Brrr. The wind blows cold off the white topped mountains. We will need to move into the government house soon." Bear Chief did not answer her.

"I must find Wise Owl and give him orders to bring in wood. The horses in the fields are growing extra-long hair; a sure sign winter is fast approaching." She walked a few steps away from Bear Chief. "Come to our tipi soon. I have been cooking special foods and we have two white men guests who want to visit with you."

Bear Chief sighed. This had been a calm, reflective evening. He didn't want to be disturbed. Flower Woman will have his bonnet and pipe at his right hand when they sit in a circle after eating. I wondered what she was up to when I hadn't seen her bustling about in the warm sun of the day. Now who can be visiting? My runners said nothing about government men in the area.

"How do you know these men?"

"I don't know them. Eagle Feather went to Browning with the

wagon for supplies. He was given the message at the trading post. He gave me the message to tell you."

"Are they government agents?"

"I do not know." Flower Woman opened the tipi flap. "Come inside with me." She teased him. "Looking Back has the children."

Bear Chief smiled as he followed her lead.

17

T HE YOUNG WARRIORS who escorted the guests to Bear Chief's tipi stood outside the flap; waited for Flower Woman to release the stick latch. The men were nervous. Neither had ever been on a reservation before. Their only instruction had been to smile a lot, try and eat the stew that was probably dog meat, and be friendly. Eagle Feather would act as the translator. He was already seated at the right arm of Bear Chief.

The light from the fire pit cast a glow upon the visitors and Flower Woman stared at the men, dressed in cloth suits and black shiny shoes. Her eyes settled upon their faces. She gasped and jumped back inside the circle. She grabbed Bear Chief's arm and in rapid Blackfoot told him of her greatest fear.

"Bear Chief! Do not let these men inside the tipi. Send them away. Tell the warriors not to touch them or their wagon or horses." She moved to stand as a guard in front of the now open flap. "Send them away. Now!"

Bear Chief saw the fear in her eyes. "What do you see Flower Woman? Did you have a message from the Great Spirit? What is frightening you?"

"These men are ill, but they do not know it yet. Look at the pocks on their faces." She shrank back into the tipi. "Do not touch them, I beg of you. They carry the sickness that killed thousands of my people when I was a child. Some of us were healed by the medicine man's herbs and prayers. I was one of them."

She pulled back her long black hair to one side. "See Bear Chief? See the scars, the marks that remained on my body? I remember Many Moons wrapping me in blankets that she had dipped in the cold Missouri River. I lay in those blankets while my teeth chattered." Flower Woman shut her eyes to try and block out that memory. "Many Moons could not save her family. She sent three of her babies down the path to the Sand Hills in two days. Only Looking Back, myself, Many Moons and two brothers were spared. The whole village lost someone to this illness."

Flower Woman looked at the two men standing outside. Each carried a Hudson Bay Wool Blanket as a gift to the Bear Chief tipi.

"Ohwee! The Government gave us infested blankets full of Small Pox; a white man's sickness. These men bring blankets." She tried to keep Bear Chief from the tipi flap.

Eagle Feather jumped to his feet. He, too, displayed the marks that he carried so many years ago. He had pock marks on his forehead and near his ears. He spoke rapid Blackfoot to Bear Chief who nodded he understood. He remembered having a very mild case when he was a young boy and that it took many seasons to gain back strength and feel strong again.

"If Flower Woman is right, this is the white man's way to rid our tribe. If it catches hold here tonight, we will be devastated. We will have to burn everything, kill our horses and dogs. The few who survive will be weak for many moons and with winter snow and cold upon us, we will lose many more throughout the village."

Bear Chief stood inside the tipi. He motioned to the two young warriors to come close. He spoke in Blackfoot as well as using sign; not wanting to alert the white men.

"Listen to your Chief. Do not touch these men or anything they might try to hand you. Do not harness their horses to the wagon. These men are not our friends. They are snakes. Take them away. Return here to me when you have sent them out of our village."

Eagle Feather stood before the bewildered men. "Bear Chief's wife is ill. She must cancel your visit. The braves will escort you out of the village." He dropped the flap and secured the stick.

"Eagle Feather, listen to your Chief."

"I am listening."

"Find my scouts. Get information. Is this a secret plan of the government? When you were in Browning last week was there talk about sickness? Find out about the illness. We have not broken any peace treaties, or made sounds with the drums that we want war. I know nothing." Bear Chief had not heard from his runners for two days and this disturbed him even more now that the white man's visit revealed so much distrust.

"**F**LOWER WOMAN, GO to Looking Back's tipi next to mine and tell her to bring Wise Owl and Little Bear with her. We will eat your dinner together. I want to talk to the sons. She is to leave the other children home."

Without asking questions, Flower Woman was out the flap and on the path to Looking Back's tipi. She called her name and the flap opened, revealing Little Bear guarding the door.

"Bear Chief wishes for you to come to eat with us. The white men are gone."

Looking Back looked surprised at the invitation but she hurried the two young men and together they left their home.

"What does father want of us? Wise Owl and I were playing a stick game and I was winning."

Flower Woman scowled. "You let our sons play that horrible game? They will learn it soon enough from the warriors." The two women and the two young braves walked towards Bear Chief's tipi where he waited on the other side of the flap.

"Welcome, my wives and my sons." He looked at Little Bear's left wrist. The scar was the only sign reminding him of the blood brother ceremony Wise Owl had done so many seasons ago. Little Bear was Blackfoot from day one; his dark eyes, black hair, and tanned skin fit the lean, athletic body. He walked, talked and understood the traditions, never knowing he was the son of a white man. He had no trouble dealing with other braves, partly because the secret had been tightly kept for years.

Bear Chief taught him well, knowing that a day for decisions would come. Wise Owl taught him to ride the wild ponies, make coup with other young men, and help Flower Woman with the brothers and sisters. He kept the wood pile full and brought fresh water every day to the tipis of both women. The boys were, in every sense of the word, blood brothers.

Wise Owl took great pride in how Little Bear listened and had instincts of a Blackfoot.

Bear Chief worried at first that Many Moons would not keep her word. He kept his promise to Flower Woman and allowed Many Moons to be a part of their family; the memories still burning deep in his mind and heart. Not even the white man's Great Spirit could change the past. Many Moons had other children who watched out for her needs. She did not come to Bear Chief's tipi unless she was invited by him.

Bear Chief ate first. He did not reach for his pipe as was his custom. "Thank you for this special dinner. I am grateful we did not share it with the white man." He smiled at her.

"Now we talk."

The women looked at each other. Looking Back waited to see if Bear Chief would speak.

Looking Back was Bear Chief's second wife. Her husband of many years was killed by a soldier in a skirmish planned by renegade Indians. He went as a warrior to try and stop the war.

Bear Chief, as was the tradition, took her and her many children as his own. She was family; she did not have a warrior to care for her; to bring her meat, or wood, or comfort in her robes. Many women were left alone and grew old and lonely after the wars ended. Bear Chief would not allow this to happen to Flower Woman's sister. They were too close to be separated in such a way.

Respectful of her sister's wishes, Looking Back kept her own tipi. Bear Chief agreed. The children would stay with Looking Back.

Bear Chief motioned for them all to sit; fill their plates with stew and chunks of bread to soak up the juices.

"Flower Woman, tonight your sharp eyes may have saved this village. Your medicine bag must have powerful spirits." He raised his arm to her. "We do not know for sure what the white man wanted, but it felt wrong to have them in our tipi."

The women looked at each other. Flower Woman told her about her fear when she saw the two government men with Hudson Bay blankets brought as gifts to Bear Chief's tipi. "Tonight we had two white man visitors wanting to speak to Bear Chief. We do not know why, or what they wanted. Eagle Feather did not have a chance to ask them questions."

Flower Woman looked into the shadows and remembered Eagle Feather had remained in the tipi. He chuckled. "Flower Woman turned into a fierce grizzly bear protecting her cub. She had me send them away."

Looking Back scowled at her sister. "This is not our way of welcome. Why did you not allow them inside the tipi?"

"Do you remember when we were very young and a horrible sickness overtook our village? We both suffered with pock marks all over our bodies that itched so badly and we had great pain?" Looking Back nodded. "We could not stop scratching. Many Moons soaked blankets in the cold river water and wrapped us up in them. I can still remember my chattering teeth and how I shook."

Flower Woman took Looking Back's hand. She looked over at the two teenaged sons. "Tonight I saw those same marks on the man at our flap. They were carrying blankets as gifts for Bear Chief." She shut her eye and clenched her hands. "Oh, I know these are not the same blankets that came up the Missouri River on steam boats many seasons ago, but the memory and fear still clings in my mind and heart." She looked over at Bear Chief. "I did not want him to touch the blankets; nor have those men inside our tipi eating our food. The Great Spirit protected us tonight; I am sure of it."

"Bear Chief smiled. "Flower Woman did the right thing. She told me in sign and in our tongue to not let them inside or touch me. Eagle Feather was here to act as a translator if needed.

He also has pock marks. He jumped in front of Flower Woman and told the men to leave; that Flower Woman had suddenly taken ill. In sign he told the young warriors not to touch anything belonging to these men; not their horses, wagon, clothes, nothing of their things. They were to make sure the men were outside the gate and down the road."

Looking Back was stunned by this news. She drew her children close, like a mother hen folds her wings over her baby chicks. The boys frowned at this kind of attention and wiggled free. Looking Back would tell them the whole story later.

"I remember the horrible smell from the stack of burning bodies. Children, women, the old and the infirm; none were spared. Thousands died in just a few weeks. The Shamans and medicine men had no power or remedy. This disease was unknown to us." A tear ran down her cheek and she brushed it away, not wanting to show emotion as that was a weakness to warriors.

Bear Chief resumed talking. "I will send Eagle Feather to Browning. He will come back with news. We will not be pushed again after all these years. The Backbone will not feed us or keep us warm in winter." Bear Chief shuddered.

"After Eagle Feather returns I will call for a meeting of the elders. We will talk to the government people. We can maybe stretch this upcoming rumor of another push for our Village and many years will pass us before action will be taken." Bear Chief remembered his medicine man telling him of a vision that came to him during a vision quest on Chief Mountain. He had never mentioned it to anyone. That vision was now coming true. The Government was taking over their land, and in turn, their people.

"I am getting weary and tired. All I ever wanted was for the nations to find peace with each other through understanding cultures and traditions."

He looked at Looking Back. "Leave now and take the sons with you. I must stay awake and prepare for a vision quest. Our Medicine Man will have what I need to carry to the top of Chief Mountain. As soon as Eagle Feather returns I will be ready to leave."

Flower Woman put her hands in her lap. She would repeat her request to go with him after Looking Back and the boys were gone. She knew women were not allowed on the mountain during a vision quest search, but she could wait at the base and pray for Bear Chief to have his quest satisfy his soul.

"Looking Back. I want you and Wise Owl and Little Bear to take care of our tipi. You are to tell no one except Eagle Feather, where I am. Five days should be time enough away."

He turned to the boys. "You are warriors now. Be alert. Do not talk to white men at the fence. Do not let anyone inside the gate. Tell any who approach we are having a fast time and cannot have guests until it is over in thirty days. They have to respect our ways."

"Yes Father. We listen to your words. Don't worry." Little Bear walked to his father's side. "Give us a blessing before we leave your tipi tonight. We do not want to carry any evil spirits back to Looking Back's tipi."

Bear Chief was surprised at the request. "My sons, you are growing into fine young warriors. With your spirits our tribe will always be protected by your gifts of wisdom, energy and ability to hear the Great Spirit and know you are being guided." He raised his arms high, stretching over both young men's heads.

Looking Back opened the flap and stepped back. She allowed the boys to leave first in front of her, showing respect for Bear Chief's words. When she stepped through the opening she looked up at the sky. Stars seemed close and extra bright.

Flower Woman watched them hurry up the well-worn path between the two tipis. She, too, looked to the heavens. *I've always believed stars are windows for our ancestors to peek through and keep track of us.* An amazing brilliance like a flaming ball of fire flashed across the sky from one mountain top only to disappear behind another making a long arc in the sky. She covered her eyes to shield them from the brightness. *Is this a sign? What does it mean?* She hurried back inside the tipi to find Bear Chief waiting to enfold her in his strong arms. He had also witnessed the phenomenon of the ball of fire blazing across the heavens. All other stars paled as if their light had been dimmed.

"Flower Woman, I want you to go with me on the Vision Quest.

I'll see to it you are safe at the base of Chief Mountain. One of our warriors will protect you from harm."

Flower Woman did not answer. She only needed to look into his eyes to see how sincere he was toward offering her the place of honor to be by his side.

19

T HE WORK AT the mission went smoothly from the first day. The homesteaders and the soldiers helped with the construction of the mission building. Men and teenaged boys joined in the building of a chapel and a home for the priests. The Blackrobes remained a mystery to the Indians; curiosity brought them closer to the project every day. The women hand sewed curtains, table clothes, pillows and pillow cases bringing color and a hominess to the rooms. Many donated furniture; table and chairs for the kitchen and two plain metal frame beds were appreciated.

The Indian women beaded beautiful garments for the two priests so they wouldn't look so drab on the altar. They used only the most special tanned soft deer hides to make elegant vestments. Some of the younger girls, helping with the hand stitching, would giggle as they worked with beads purchased or traded from Bent's Fort. Ribbons, considered a prize possession, were donated gladly to add color and festivity to the garments. The priests were humbled by these acts of love and acceptance from them.

"How beautiful." Father Jerome slipped into a vestment that fit him perfectly. He raised his right hand and blessed the ladies with the sign of the cross. "We will be the most handsomely decorated men at the next rendezvous." He winked at the youngest girls just to hear their happy giggle. The garment he wore had at least 50 elk teeth decorating the front, and a tightly woven sash of many colors wrapped around his waist. "How splendid I am going to look at Sunday's services." He smiled and turned around in a circle. "Please tell your neighbors to come and see us."

Father Michael, used to many years of wearing the simple garments of black, shifted his eyes upward. "Harrumph! You don't expect me to wear one of those costumes, do you?"

"Yes, of course I do; yes, you will wear the vestment this Sunday." Father Jerome turned to the three Indian women who expected a smile from Father Michael. They looked sad and disappointed by his response.

"Don't fret, ladies. He will be splendid on Sunday. I'll see to it that he practices wearing it so he can get used to how the vestment feels. We are not familiar with such splendor."

"Whoa there, hoses." The muscular horse obeyed but not before it gave a nicker of a greeting. A rather large black woman jumped from the wagon box and came in to the group's view. "Howdy there Padres; ladies." She tipped her battered straw hat that shielded her eyes from the hot sun as she drove her mail route, picking up canisters of milk, eggs, chickens; anything left along the roadside. Homesteaders counted on her to deliver and pick up in all kinds of weather.

"Hello to you, too, Mary. Do you bring us mail?" Father Jerome looked forward to visiting with Mary Fields. She laughed away her troubles in that deep-from-the-belly kind of laugh that southerners possessed. She also knew how to fix most anything that needed fixing around the mission.

"Howdy Fathers." She dug into her potato sack and pulled out some envelopes. "This one I almost opened myself. Laws, it says it's from the Bishop in Helena, Montana. Now what do you suppose he wants?"

Father Jerome took the letter and out of respect for the older priest, he handed it to him to open and read it first.

"Harrumph." His eyes grew wider with each sentence. "Oh! My!"

"What is it, Father? Please may I read the letter now?"

"The older priest folded the letter and put it in his pocket. "Not now. No."

Perplexed, Father Jerome politely showed the women outside. Usually when company came to the Mission he would serve tea or lemonade (if he had lemons) but this day he was in a hurry to be alone to read the unexpected letter. What on earth does the Bishop want from us? Surely he has heard only good things. The Indians are helping us; no renegades have burned us out, or trampled our gardens. How am I going to know what the letter says if Father keeps it hidden inside his pocket?"

The worst thoughts crowded into his head. What if he is transferring us to another place; sending us back east? We have been here for so many years. We have plans to open a boarding house for young women; to educate the Indians in white man's ways. Maybe we have become too lax in our priestly duties? I must find Father Michael. He has retired to his room; hopefully he is still awake. Father Jerome hurried to the back side of the wood and rock house they called the mission house.

"Father, please, may I read the letter?"

The older man lifted his hands to his chest. He pulled out the envelope containing the mysterious letter and held it up to Father Jerome.

"Here." His arm dropped back to the bed cover. "You read it, but sit down first."

Father Jerome took the letter and sat in his very plain wood chair near his small desk that Father Michael used as his office space.

The silence in the room was palpable. "Oh! My!" Father Jerome kept reading, making strange sounds as he did so. "Well, we just have to prepare everyone and Sunday I will make an announcement." Where do I begin, what do I say? What will the reaction be from those in attendance at Mass? This is certainly unexpected, but we have faced challenges and came through with the Lord's help. We can remain calm, be positive, and trust the Bishop knows what is best for us. This can be a very good advance for us and for the mission itself. Maybe we can raise money for repairs? Sunday all of our lives, our hopes and dreams, will change forever.

Father Jerome placed the letter on the little table. "Keep track of this letter, Father. It will be one to keep in our history journal and will be read over and over through the years that this mission is in place. I need a walk outside."

Father Jerome walked toward the barn and met, of all people, Mary Fields. Obviously, she had stayed in the yard, curious about the letter. She looked very worried when she saw the Blackrobe coming toward her.

"Laws, Father Jerome. You's don' look so good. What's eat'n away at you's? Somethin' in that letter I brung?"

"Hello, Mary. Why am I not surprised to see you here?" The priest put his arm on the fence gate and his foot on a rung and looked out into the meadow. He didn't know how much to visit with Mary about the letter but she certainly would be involved in whatever came down that path.

"I've got a feelin'. Some good, some bad." She stared at the man, waiting for him to say something. He did not respond to her nudges. "The Bishop comin' here soon? He's never been here in all these years. I picked up a letter from Fort Shaw that got sent in the mail to the Bishop in Helena, Montana about a month ago. Didn' say nothin' 'cause it ain't none of my business. Besides it weren't somethin' one brings up in a friendly hello kind of talkin'."

"You are quite right, Mary. The Bishop is planning to visit us very soon. We are going to have to do a lot of fixing up around here before he arrives. Do you think you can pull a crew together?"

"Probably most the stuff I kin do. But, yes, the outside will look sharp. You goin' to tell the crowd Sunday?"

"Yes, at the end of Mass. I'll ask for women volunteers to help me get the rooms ready for the Bishop. His driver and team and wagon can go on down the road to the fort where they have room for guests. The Bishop wants to spend his time with us." Father Jerome sighed. "That means Father and I will sleep in the hay in the barn. I can hear the older priest grumbling already, can't you?"

"He don' mean nothin' with all the harrumphing he does. It is a habit for him after all these years. Why, he tol' me jes this mornin' this is home and he has picked out a plot in the Christian section of the cemetery up on the knoll so he can overlook the com'n and go'n of the mission."

Father Jerome laughed out loud. "Why, that's very funny, Mary. Thank you for telling me. However he knows that will not happen. We have a cemetery at our main seminary that we will wind up in one day." He shrugged. "I just don't want to be transferred away from here.

I love this life, as hard as it is, Mary. We have accomplished something; carved a bit of Montana history in our own fashion."

"I feel the same, Father. It would be hard for me to leave here, too. Sister Amadeus and I have been friends for years. She brought me out here when she was so sick with that coughing disease and I jes' forgot to leave." She frowned. "I wonder what the Bishop will do or say when he meets me."

I wonder about that too, Mary. "Well, let's not borrow trouble until trouble borrows us." *This part of the country needs this mission. Maybe a letter writing campaign to the Bishop and to the man in Washington who is in charge of the Religions settling in? If only we had the boarding house and school finished. The town of Fort Shaw has their own parish to support, so we need government money to keep us afloat. Maybe I've been too cautious in my spending habits, trying to be conservative?*

20

*M*ARY HAD WATCHED *the priest walk out into the field. She heard his favorite old horse nickering. He always has sugar cubes in his pocket for that critter. My goodness, that horse must be the oldest living animal in the country. She smiled as she watched the communication of love spread between human and animal. That horse has the best life. Gets to eat grass all day; has a lump of sugar and doesn't do any work to earn it. Well, that isn't quite true. He gives the young'uns some happiness when he lets them crawl all over him. I saw an Injun boy sliding down his neck just the other day. The horse seemed to like the attention, too, dropping his head and swinging the boy up onto his bare back.*

The priest patted his old friend and gave him the expected lump of sugar. "You are going to have some company in this meadow. I want you to behave; no kicking at the Bishop's horse, now, you hear?"

The old nag nickered and swung his head up and down, as if to let Father Jerome know he heard. As the priest continued walking through the grass, the horse kept in step until they reached the gate. "Thanks for the walk and the conversation, old friend. I hope I get the same cooperation Sunday from the congregation." He patted the horse on its rump and with a renewed energy and attitude, returned to the mission house.

He had work to do; Father Michael would have to be excited about this Bishop's first visit. We have been very creative working on a shoestring to bring this mission into existence. It would be a tragedy to see it taken away from these people who have depended upon the faith to be here to console and feed their very souls. I need to check our baptismal records to see how many have joined the faithful over the past fifteen years.

Mary sat on a wooden bench, thankful for the shady side of the house. She waited for the good Blackrobe to approach.

"Why Mary; you are still here? I thought you'd be to the fort with their mail by now."

"I'm not leavin' 'til I's know what's in that letter. Why is the Bishop himself comin' here?"

"From what I gather, Mary, he is coming to help us celebrate our anniversary for all these years we've been together. I will have more communication with him, hopefully. In fact, will you stop by in the morning? I'll have a letter for you to mail post-haste back to the Bishop." He smiled at the black woman who so faithfully helped around the mission. She had a little homesteader type house to live in at the edge of the property. Everyone passed by her place either coming or going. She knew most of the gossip from those who stopped to chat.

"Please, Mary, keep this one under your hat until Sunday. I have some planning to do before I make the big announcement."

"Why you's don't have to ask me twice. Jes be sure I hear it first, okay?"

They both laughed, enjoying the moment.

"Gotta skedaddle; people want their mail."

Father Jerome watched Mary as she went on her way to deliver the rest of her load.

Mary liked her life. She helped Mother Amadeus, her best friend in all the world, with mission work. The first building after the Mission House was a small barn that housed animals, stored hay, and had nests for the chickens. Father Jerome planned to turn it into a boarding school for boys. The enrollment was higher than expected as the homesteaders were happy to have their boys learning to read and write English; study math, and learn about the world.

That successful venture now launched the idea of building a boarding school for girls. Three Ursaline sisters were scheduled to come soon. *Maybe that is what the Bishop is checkin' out. They can teach the girls how not to be like me.* Mary laughed that deep belly laugh; her horse kept on plodding down the rutted road as if he hadn't heard her.

Mary had a questionable reputation. She liked to drink, smoke, cuss, work like a man, shoot wild game, live in her little cabin, and drive the postal wagon in all four seasons and all kinds of weather. This year she would have chalked up over 8 years as the postal worker; never missing a day of delivery. *It still makes me smile in wonder at her friendship with Sister Amadeus for all these years. Maybe somebody has complained to the Bishop and he'll get rid of me. Then what will I do?* For a minute Mary was confused and fearful for her future at the Mission. *God has taken care of me this far; He ain't goin' to cut me loose now.*

Father Jerome waited until Mary had left the yard, closing the gate behind her, saving her the jolting jump to the ground to shut the gate. They waved to each other; she going on down the road; he walking into the mission house. *I like that woman. She has a good heart for everyone she meets.* The screen door slammed behind him. *Now to talk with Father about this new wrinkle in our otherwise scheduled routine.*

"There you are. I believe I'd like a cup of tea with you. We have an exciting month ahead of us, don't you agree?" He went to the tea pot, felt its lid and decided it was still hot. He found his mug and filled it with the brew. "This just hits the spot. I needed some liquid after my walk in the meadow." He sat down on a wood chair next to the other priest. "Where do we begin?" He took a sip of tea; reached for a pencil and note book nearby.

"Have you had some delightful thoughts about entertaining the Bishop here in our humble abode?"

"Harrumph! Call it what you like. Yes, I have been thinking about a welcoming committee, with Blackfoot Indians in costume beating on their drums; Union soldiers from Fort Shaw making an honor guard wearing their fancy hats, parade uniforms, and swords." He took a gulp of tea. "We can send invitations to Bear Chief up there in the Glacier country since they were here when we started this Mission. Have a few tipis set up, have a fancy dinner at the fort one evening. Things like that."

"My goodness, you have wonderful and colorful ideas to show the Bishop what it is like here. The weather is usually good that time of the season so people can travel. Maybe I can get a beaded pair of moccasins made for the Bishop to wear when he says Mass. We will wear our beaded vestments, and the Indian ladies will want to dress as if going to a rendezvous. They will bring their native foods, of course. We can set up a food line in the yard out front.

"Will you say the Mass this Sunday?"

"I thought you wanted to."

'No. I want the time to make the announcement and to openly talk about the importance of this visit."

"Fine. I'll be prepared for the sermon, too. Do you suppose we should plan a communal baptism down at the Sun River?"

"Splendid idea. Yes, indeed. We have given out enough instruction, and the young people can help with dunking the heads into the river water."

Father Jerome clapped his hands together. He stretched his fingers as if they were cramped from all the writing down of ideas. "A parade from the fort to the Sun River Crossing would be a wonderful sight for children to see. There would be Soldiers, Indians, farmers, homesteaders, business people from the town; drummers and the Army band." Father Jerome reached his still cramped fingers around the pencil and continued to write all the new ideas.

"This will be a drawing of dignitaries from the community, homesteaders, Indians, soldiers, priests, strangers meeting others, and friends visiting with people they have not seen for some time." He drank the rest of his cup of tea. "I don't know why we didn't do this years ago."

He grew solemn and looked over at his long-time friend and mentor. "Father, what if he is coming here for other reasons? Like maybe to tell us he is closing the mission, that we will be transferred back east? What then?"

Father Michael read the anguish in Father Jerome's face.

"Then we will do as directed. If it means we leave here, then God must need us elsewhere. Just as we were sent here so long ago now, it seems, maybe we have completed what we were intended to do. Mission accomplished, move on to start another one." He drew in a breath.

"I have to admit, I won't be happy to leave here. This has become our family. But if we are to be seed planters and not harvest pickers, then so be the will of our Lord." With that long speech, Father Michael arose and turned his head so the younger man could not see the tears that were ready to spill out. "We can only wait and see where this mysterious visit takes us." He walked to the front door. "I, too, need to take a walk. I'll be in the garden for a while. The corn stalks need tending." He left the building.

<h1 style="text-align:center">21</h1>

EAGLE FEATHER RETURNED the next evening. His horse had sensed the urgency and Eagle Feather used secret trails known only to his people. They only stopped for water whenever they crossed a small creek. He went straight to Bear Chief's tipi and scratched on the flap. The strong scent of coffee lured him like a Lorelei that tempts the sailors in the great oceans of the world.

"Eagle Feather. Enter. You made good time. What is the government up to now? Do we need to be concerned?"

Eagle Feather smiled at Flower Woman as she handed him a cup of steaming coffee. *Whatever herbs and berries she grinds together makes for a good drink.* He took a sip and it burned his tongue.

"Bear Chief, the big news in Bent's Fort is that the Bishop from Helena is going to visit in the next full moon." Eagle Feather took a biscuit that Flower Woman handed to him.

"Why is the Bishop visiting; where is he going to stay?"

"You remember years ago when the Blackrobes came up the Missouri to start a Mission? The Bishop will stay with them."

Bear Chief nodded his head. "Yes. We were living there at that time, until the government pushed us to the backbone country." Bear Chief's eye squinted as he stared into the fire pit.

"A meeting, like a rendezvous, is going to happen with dancing and food and many people." Eagle Feather laughed. "Much white man talk. You will be invited; *expected* to attend. A letter is on its way to you as we speak. You will be asked to talk about the move."

"We pick up and move back? Near the Union fort?"

"Not this time."

"No. You will speak about how our village was dying until the government came in to save us." Eagle Feather coughed from laughter.

"You are to be a part of this event. The priests will announce this news at their Sunday service. They will have a day for baptisms in the Sun River. White man wedding services and many Masses on the list. They will ask for help from the people to plan the weeks of events and activities. Big time fun." He laughed. "We will have to be the savage Blackfoot Nation of the past; better get your face paint and war bonnet ready to go." Laughter filled the tipi and spilled out into the open air.

"Little Bear and Wise Owl will lead the younger families who do not remember those days. I will translate for us when you are asked to speak. That is if you trust me to not use a forked tongue."

Bear Chief stared at Eagle Feather. Flower Woman poured them both more coffee. She wanted to hear more. She looked to the floor so the men could not see her smiling. *What good news; something for me to look forward to being with family once more. Of course we will go.*

"I'll not take part." Bear Chief stood firm. He crossed his chest with folded arms.

"What? Of course we will go." Flower Woman knew better than to argue in front of Eagle Feather but this was important news. "Eagle Feather will go with us."

"Stop. I'll do whatever Bear Chief asks of me." He drained the cup. "I leave now. You talk. Word spreads fast. Our people want something outside this reservation fence." He walked to the open flap on the tipi. "We must show respect for the white man ways. Maybe we can have a rogue band of warriors come in and ride ponies through the crowd, lances painted with red blood?" Eagle Feather stepped back outside. "I'll take the Bishop captive and tie him to a tree."

Bear Chief stood close to Flower Woman. "He still didn't tell me what the two men with blankets wanted from us. Listen to me Flower Woman. Never trust someone bearing gifts. They put one nose into the tipi and soon they step inside. I must take time and pray about this."

Flower Woman picked up a packed parfleche. "We must leave at once for your spirit quest. Your needs and confusion mounts each day you delay."

"I sent one of my guards to set up a camp at the base of Chief Mountain for you. You will be safe from wild animals and any human predators looking for off-reservation Indians to shoot."

"Thank you for that, Bear Chief. I only want to spend this time with you and share prayers with the Great Spirit. You will not have to worry about me. Nothing will harm me while waiting for your return from the top of the sacred mountain."

"The horses are ready. Wise Owl has gone to tend to them. Little Bear has already spoken to me and he waits your return to visit with you about your quest."

Bear Chief opened the tent flap. "The fire has burned down to ashes. Little Bear will sleep here while we are gone." He motioned to Flower Woman to leave the tipi.

—⟡—⟡—⟡—⟡—

22

T HE OLD MAN, bent at the waist, stepped out of his cave into the warm sunshine. Years earlier, even before he was released of his post and retired as the commander of Fort Shaw, he had found this solid granite deep cave; midway, up the side of the hill. Eagles built nests in the pine trees and nearby cottonwood trees surrounding it. He listened for their screech when they dove for the water. Fish swimming in the river below kept the birds well-fed.

Water from the Missouri never rose high enough to flood the cave's floor during high water season and a path of hardened red clay lead to the river's edge. The climb was easy for the old man and animals used the path as much as he did. Carrying water buckets back to the cave for his personal use was not a chore for him. At least not yet. Chopping ice during the extremely cold months was his hardest chore; he didn't mind since he liked to drop a line into the hole and grab a fresh fish for his meal that day.

Near the sunny side of the land he cultivated a wonderful vegetable garden, spending several early morning hours tending to it; hunting for wild game came easy since the deer followed the clay path nature provided for them to find water. He also had a pole corral with a lean-to shelter for the one horse he rode when he went to town for supplies. Usually in the fall he'd take a ride back to the fort to meet with a few other retired soldiers. Guards at Fort Shaw always welcomed him; waved him on through the gates.

He planned to live in his cave the rest of his life. It was quite comfortable for him. He kept a good supply of books on a shelf, buying and trading books at Bent's Fort. The mountain men liked to trade off their books, too. An assortment of newspapers most outdated but of interest to read, held a place of honor on the book shelf.

He had the river to keep a few items cold. Handy and clever at making useful items, he had fashioned an open-slatted basket from some wire he had found years ago, abandoned on the trail. This fit snugly into the hole he had dug in the shallow water at the edge of the river bank and lined it with rock.

He used huge iron mining bolts pushed into the hard rock walls to hang his hat, a pistol kept in a leather cartridge belt, and the buffalo coat he wore in the cold season. He stored his nicer clothes in dresser drawers along with his handwritten Will. He rarely wore civilian clothes. He had left the fort in Union blues made from good wool; these clothes he still wore every day, weaving threads into patches as needed; the boots he cut tanned hide when resoling was necessary. He preferred to wear his hand-made moccasins most of the time. They were simple to cut, using leather scraps for the soles and ties. He wore the same underwear all winter season, taking them off in the spring long enough to dunk them into the river for a scrub; drying the garment by tossing it onto the pine tree branch to let the sun dry things out. The same for his body; a dunk now and then in the river was all the old fellow needed. He semi-hibernated the winter days, staying inside the cave, sleeping, reading, and wondering how it had come to this way of life.

When he was younger and owned more strength and energy, many of his faithful soldiers came by to check on him. They had cut a cottonwood tree with a huge two-man saw that he'd traded for in Bent's Fort to make circles for a table top and chair seats. These chairs still held firm and the thick slice made the perfect sized table top. It served him well for a kitchen set and a good place to sit and visit while drinking his homemade hooch. He liked making beer when he could get supplies to do so. He smiled whenever he'd open a Mason jar filled to the top with the 'Fruit of the Gods'; wine made from his very own garden where grapes and dandelions both grew in profusion. But his favorite was making poteen from potatoes, just like his Irish mother had taught him. A kerosene lamp hung on a hook from the ceiling.

A smaller table he had placed near his bed. He preferred to use candles. Lucifer sticks were bartered when he traded hides each spring. The candles were very large in size and gave off a bright glow when he wanted to read into the night. He entertained himself by watching shadows from the flickering flame when he couldn't fall asleep. Sometimes, even after all these years, he still could not shake the memory of his wife's disappearance. He had several faithful old dogs over the years; his only companions.

The only memento of that time was a large square of calico material that had somehow been ripped from her dress and one high-button black shoe left tangled in the barbs on the bushes. These items he stored in a seldom opened trunk resting on a rock ledge in the back of the cave. It gave him peace to live in his cave; as if she was near; forgiving him for not saving her.

Every time I go to Bent's Fort and see an Indian I wonder all over again. Did that Indian tribe seen on the ridge kidnap her and the newborn? The Utes took their captives to Mexico and sold them for big money. They were slaves to rich Mexican landowners until they finally were released; died. It has been 16 years of grief and despair. Where is she? Where is my son? No answer ever came riding the rushing water; only more questions and anguish.

Needing a rest, the old man sat on his tree stump outside the entrance, and stared at the river; always the river taking his thoughts; cleansing his mind; trying to mend his shattered heart. This day, however, his restlessness was bringing on a headache, something he did not want to deal with.

Guess I'll ride on into town and get some news. It's time to get some more flour and coffee. He hobbled over to the corral, whistled to his horse to come to him.

"Come on, old boy, let's you and me go for a ride. Time to saddle up." I've got a couple of nice cat hides with a good fur; guess they'll do for a solid trade. Sure wish old Bent still run the place. The new owners don't know

how to deal with us old traders. But I'll keep taking what I can get to keep me going. I better get a sack of oats for old faithful out there in the yard.

He wrote down his needs and looked at his growing list. I best take the wagon to bring back this much supplies. It won't hurt to stock up on pantry things, too. One thing's for sure. Fall surprises us all when she comes early; when I'll be needin' them extra stuff. Food? Now that's a different problem. Sure glad I have my garden and my dug out where I can store vegetables. Been doing it now for a long, long time. Better get in more coffee in case I get some company. He let out a roaring laugh. As if company ever finds me in my hidey-hole.

City people don't have a clue as to how many of us live in caves all along this river. One thing the Indians did when they left was leave us white men their cache caves. I remember the bundles I found; best jerky I ever ate, and I ate them all that first winter. He quickly reached for his pencil and paper. I like canned tomatoes. Need some salt and spices, too.

The horse stood by the wagon parked near the gate. He pawed the ground as if to say, let's get going, old man. I need some exercise and so do you.

The hides were rolled and tied; an ax, and an extra wheel hung from an iron hook, tied with twine on the right side; some rope coiled up on the floor. The harness slid easily over the horse's head; reins stretched across his rump. The old man climbed into the wagon, slapped the reins once and the wheels made their first turn in the hard clay ground. "Yahoo! He shouted. Here we go."

23

B EAR CHIEF AND Flower Woman made good time riding the very best horses in their corral.

The weather held and a blue Montana sky brightened their spirits as they cantered side by side. Flower Woman spotted smoke and veered her horse in that direction.

"That must be where I will be staying, Bear Chief. That is near the base of the mountain where you plan to make your vision quest. You have been to the top several times but I am asking you to stay with me this night so we talk about what the Great Spirit has to tell you; what He wants you to do for your health and for our Village. You used to climb this mountain, never feeling shortness of breath. Now you have to go slower, breathe harder."

Bear Chief whistled a loud screech, alerting the guard they were near the camp. He heard a return screech and kicked his horse in the ribs leaving Flower Woman behind.

I love watching him when he is feeling like a young warrior brave, like when I first saw him. We have shared seasons longer than even I can remember. She stopped her horse and stared at the beautiful view stretching ahead of her. The long shadow from the mountain cast designs in the grasses; trees and bushes looked elongated on the earth. Everything exuded peace.

Flower Woman saw a covey of birds pick up and leave their hiding places. Something had disturbed them but they only circled and resettled themselves.

Suddenly the sky darkened and a huge cloud of bees approached her. She shielded her eyes and as they grew closer she recognized the insect. *Those are not bees. They are butterflies; black and yellow Monarch butterflies. One of my spirit guides.* She held out her arm and hoped the butterflies would land on her clothes. They did not disappoint her. One very large butterfly landed on the top of her hand and closed its wings as if to sleep. It remained with her until she could no longer hold out her arm. The butterflies settled in the near bushes. To Flower woman they looked like fluttering leaves hanging from the branches.

Bear Chief looked back for her. When he saw the happy smile, he knew something special had occurred and he motioned her to come forward.

Flower Woman rode into camp and jumped from her horse's back. She pointed to a huge fluffy cloud that looked like a giant mushroom, hanging above them. "Thank goodness that is not a rain cloud forming. Look how the clouds are changing color to purple and pinks. The sunset will be outstanding, Bear Chief. Father Sky is welcoming you."

Flower Woman laid her head on Bear Chief's shoulder.

Bear Chief laughed. He put his right arm around his woman. That one moment of tenderness filled Flower Woman's heart, turning it into a lasting memory.

"From the ground when we look up to the top of Chief Mountain it looks flat." He moved his left arm into a half-circle. "It is full of surprises. Grass is thin, yes, but still it fights to grow flowers so there is beauty for a warrior seeking a vision quest. Rain comes and waters it. I remember seeing rain falling just over this mountain when I was a boy. It looked like a very large bucket full of water being dumped out. I promise you I will not fall off the edge."

Flower Woman found peace as she watched the golden hues from the falling sun.

"Soon it will be dark. Do you think you will have a spirit guide visitor tonight?"

He took a breath. "I always see my bear when I come here."

Flower Woman turned her head and pondered her thoughts; she folded her fingers into the palm of her hand and struck her heart two times.

I wonder where the guard is hiding? When will the medicine man join us? Tonight? In the morning? I see we have wood for at least four days. The guard was to prepare the vision quest space with wood. Maybe he is on top now. I'll not concern myself with his presence tonight. I'll be near Bear Chief.

They passed the night, shielded from a brisk wind that had come up. Bear Chief shouted his prayers to the Great Spirit to send his spirit guide; to give him advice. He watched for any sign of a bear.

Flower Woman prayed in silence. They finally dozed off in each other's arms, feeling comfort that this coming day would bring the answers they sought.

The breaking of dawn was so beautiful that tears filled Flower Woman's eyes. Neither was hungry. They did drink water from the canteen, but were careful to not lose a drop of the precious liquid.

Bear Chief heard a grunting noise and he jumped to his feet. Not more than a stone's throw away stood his magnificent Grizzly; the sun shining through the bristle-hairs the wind had ruffled up. "Thank you Great Spirit for sending me my spirit guide this morning."

"See the bear? I am to follow him. I have my Vision Quest pack and the blanket our medicine man gave me to cover my nakedness during the cold nights." He undressed leaving his clothes in a pile at Flower Woman's feet. He chose to wear his moccasins up the trail. "I've been studying with our medicine man for over a year now. I am ready."

Bear Chief turned his palms toward the bear that stood very still, watching his every move. "I thank you Bear for climbing the trail in front of me. You have never failed me."

Flower Woman remained silent. Bear Chief never looked back. The bear loped easily across the grasses forcing Bear Chief to run to stay with him.

Flower Woman sat down on a large boulder. Quietly, she said her own prayer of thanksgiving. Dear Heavenly Father, thank you for sending Bear

Chief his sign. He will be able to make decisions for the village when we return. Our children are safe; the white man's plans will be discovered and no harm will come to our tribe. Please have Bear Chief see the need for our attending the festivities at Fort Shaw. There is something in Your plans that we don't know of, but You will reveal it all in Your precious time. Amen.

The trail proved to be more difficult than Bear Chief remembered it. He stopped to rest at every twist in the trail, keeping in sight of the bear ahead. The pack slung over his shoulder grew heavier as he went higher. Oxygen lessened in his lungs making it harder to breathe. *Do not look down, only look up. With each step you are closer to the top. Move only one foot at a time and pace yourself. There is no reason to rush. You are here. The bear is here. Father Sky has welcomed you.* Bear Chief kept thinking his thoughts taught him by the healer.

Flower Woman took a basket and wandered in the direction of where she had seen the birds. She looked carefully beneath the bushes hoping to find eggs in a nest. She also picked service berries that were ripe for the season of picking. The morning passed quickly. She had no fears of being alone; the guard still had not come into camp. She knew where he was by looking for smoke from his cooking fire. He would hear her cry out if she was in trouble. He also could see her movements. Bear Chief had assigned him to keep watch from a distance, but move swiftly if trouble came to her.

Flower Woman scanned the mountain late in the afternoon. Much to her relief, she saw smoke billowing from the top. *As long as there is smoke, Bear Chief is fine. I'll watch for smoke.*

Tonight he will be wrapped in his blanket to ward off the chill. I will do the same. I'll wrap up in a robe and face the mountain. My prayers and watchful eyes will go ever upward until Father Sky sees and covers Bear Chief. He will be safe.

It was late afternoon when Bear Chief reached the top of Chief Mountain. He had work to do before darkness overtook him. He opened his Vision Quest pack and pulled out four stakes, each flying a flag of a different color; red, white, black and yellow. He thought he heard rustling of a bush nearby and immediately he saw his spirit guide, stretched out in his direction, watching him set up the sacred ceremonial objects provided by the medicine man.

Bear Chief had no fear of the bear. They had been through many years together. His name from birth had given him the courage to always welcome the bear when seen on hunting trips. His favorite neck piece was a bear claw; the long nails bent in a protective statue-like shape. He wore it for all ceremonials. His mother, many seasons ago when he was a baby had threaded a slim piece of leather thong through the nails. It was long enough to circle his neck behind his head.

A large square of heavy cloth Bear Chief spread on the ground. He pounded in the four flags stakes, one in each corner. This would be his allotted space and he must not leave that space. The wood pile and fire pit were within his reach for when he needed a fire to light the tobacco stored in the sacred pipe. He respected this pipe handmade many seasons ago by Eagle Feather. The hollow pipe represented the hollow man. Many moons ago the medicine man had accepted the pipe and became connected to Bear Chief spiritually, physically and mentally. Bear Chief would concentrate on that friendship and leadership while on the mountain.

The darkness enveloped Bear Chief as he wrapped his naked body with the blanket. He sat cross-legged in the center of the cloth. He thought of Flower Woman but had no fear for her safety. One of his best guards was assigned to watch out for her and keep her safe. They had a secret signal should the need arise for Bear Chief to leave the mountain.

A cold wind blew. The bear moved closer to the man. This was a comfort to Bear Chief, knowing no harm would come to him.

Bear Chief looked to the dark but cloudless sky. He was surprised to see how close he was to the stars; especially the Big Dipper. The cup seemed full but slightly tipped. Something liquid was flowing down from Father Sky and splashing on Mother Earth. Bear Chief held up his hands in a cup shape pretending to catch the liquid but he could not stop the flow. The colorless liquid leaked through his fingers determined to end up where it was meant to be sent. He welcomed the warm liquid but did not taste it. He would not break his fast.

Thank you Father Sky for my first sign. I am to travel in a south direction soon. That would be the festival at the St. Peter's Mission. Flower Woman will be happy about this trip. She wants to see where we lived many years ago and where our son is buried. I'll see to that. Just then a very cold wind blew over Bear Chief. Nothing else moved that was clinging to Mother Earth. What is coming out of the north? Something I must be prepared to accept? The wind blows very cold.

The breaking of dawn was peaceful. Flower Woman woke and stretched in her robe. The birds singing, movement in the grasses, sunlight casting golden light over her camp brought tears to her eyes. She took a drink from her canteen but did not eat food. The fire burned ashes all night long. Without Flower Woman being aware, the guard had snuck in and tended to her fire, not making a sound. The horses did not nicker a welcome even when the guard poured some oats on the ground for the animals.

Bear Chief did not move his body, but he felt the sun's warmth as he woke into the world from somewhere deep in sleep. *"Thank you Great Spirit for my safety last night.* He put his canteen to wet his lips but did not drink, not wanting to break his fast the first day. *You have never failed me.*

The day wore on as Bear Chief said the required prayers to the Great Spirit. He performed all the ceremonial moves to fulfill his quest. He asked the Great Spirit for answers to his many questions; confusing and cluttering his mind over the past few moons. One repeated prayer he desperately wanted an answer. *What are your plans for the future of our Nation?*

Flower Woman watched for smoke throughout the second and third day. Time hurried through her camp. She took short naps, and spent hours in prayer asking for answers that bothered Bear Chief. *Will you tell him the future or will we just have to live each day and recognize the answers as they approach our Village?*

Trying to stay awake caused Bear Chief to weaken in body and spirit. He found himself taking short naps, only to be awakened by a grunt from the bear that never left his side. Each time this happened Bear Chief would ask, "Do you have a message for me?" Sometimes the bear shook his head up and down. "I will have to wait and see what it is? You will not leave my side until the Great Spirit releases you?" The bear once again shook his head up and down.

Bear Chief felt his body weakening. His legs were stiff, and he was losing reality. He took a log and poked at the fire, spreading the burnt logs so there would be no more smoke. Today I leave the mountain. I have peace in my heart. If I am ill, then it is nature's way of preparing me through the pain that grips my side. The future is going to be a mystery and a journey for me to take. I am content. Patience will guide me, along with Flower Woman by my side. Looking Back will see to our children. Eagle Feather will protect them in my place. It is done.

Flower Woman glanced up one more time looking for smoke. When she saw none, she knew Bear Chief would be leaving the sacred ground and return to his chiefly duties. True to tradition he would share his vision with her today; maybe never. But he would be a changed man with new energy and directions for his people. She saw her guard working his way down the trail. He was half-carrying Bear Chief. They would be in camp very soon. Flower Woman built up her fire and put berries and herbs into a pot. She wanted to make a healing broth for Bear Chief. He would not want a big meal right away. She intended to pack boiled eggs, bread and water. Duck Lake would be the place to stop for a break for her and for him. She would not want to eat a meal before then. *Maybe Bear Chief will tell me of his vision when we stop to eat.*

It took a while to reach Flower Woman. Bear Chief immediately sat cross-legged on a bear rug on the ground. He seemed to be in a fog, maybe hallucinating? Flower Woman could not understand what he was trying to tell her. She spooned the herbal broth into his mouth and forced him to swallow. He fell onto his back with a huge sigh and shut his eyes.

Flower Woman was very concerned and she turned to the guard. "If he isn't strong enough to ride, we will stay here one more night. Do you know where the medicine man is?"

"Yes. He is near. But Bear Chief only needs rest and food. You'll see him soon with energy after this nap. He is in need of oxygen. You can pack. I'll tend to your horses. I will not leave you alone." The guard moved to the other side of the tent and to shield himself from the hot sun. He also needed water and shade.

24

F ATHER MICHAEL LOOKED splendid in his beaded vestments as he finished saying Mass to an over-crowded congregation. He smiled as he turned to Father Jerome.

"And now, Father Jerome has some announcements. Please stay in your seats and on the lawn. It is nice to see so many of you participating in the Mass celebration with me today."

Father Jerome, a letter in hand, walked to the altar and faced the crowd.

"I have good news and want to share it with you." He held up the letter. Mary Fields, standing near the entrance of the tent, waved to him. "Our Stagecoach Mary delivered the most surprising letter to the Mission about five days ago." He pointed his hand towards Mary. She took a bow and people clapped.

Mary Fields, a rough-and-tumble kind of black lady from Tennessee, had a heart as big as the Montana Territory. Most of the people in the valley knew of her ways: drinking, cursing, hunting, chewing, dressing in leather pants, and shooting guns; the list of her sins seemed to grow longer each season. She was faithful to the Mission, and Sister Amadeus was grateful for her presence at the boarding school. She could fix anything, passing her abilities and skills on to the boys. They respected her and were happy to work with her on the various projects at the Mission.

Father Jerome adjusted his gold-rimmed glasses and started to read the letter. When he read the sentence about the upcoming visit from the Bishop in Helena, a gasp went up as if one person alone had heard him.

"Read that again, Father. You say the Bishop is coming here? Why? When?"

"Let me finish the letter." He dropped his eyes to the white sheet of paper and started over from the top. No one moved from their spot, or spoke a word.

"What I am asking from you is that you help us to host this special member of the clergy.

I don't know *why* he is coming, but I assume he wants to see what we are doing here. Maybe he will be bringing us a sack full of gold so we can build the boarding school for girls?" No one laughed at his attempt to make a joke. "Maybe someone has written a complaint."

Ahah! Just as I thought, the homesteader's wife from New Jersey looks grim. Instead of coming to me, she must have written the Bishop something he didn't need to read. She could have come directly to me or to Father Michael instead of stirring up trouble. Well, we'll just have to wait and see. Father Jerome continued his announcement.

This will be the first time for the Bishop to visit us. It is a long trip from Helena, as you all know." Several heads nodded in agreement. "What I am asking is cooperation and volunteers so we can have an anniversary celebration with the fort participating; invite Bear Chief and the Blackfoot reservation to bring tipis and set up a camp. We can have a rendezvous type of party." The good priest smiled. "This will take time from your already busy schedules, but it also will provide first-hand information showing the good Bishop what the Mission is all about."

He read some more of the letter. "This will take place in three weeks from now. The Bishop will stay at the Mission, but it would be wonderful if you ladies could invite him for dinner. Let him see what homesteading is really all about. He can watch you cook the vegetables from your gardens, and eat country-fried chicken. He will have his own driver, of course." Several women clapped their hands and were turning to others already forming plans.

Father Michael stood up and faced the crowd. "Let's take a day to think about what job you could handle. I'll have note paper handy and you can come by and write down what you would like to do, for example, help with set-ups of long-table meals out on the lawn. Men, we will need your help in setting up those tables and bringing chairs and benches."

The women were poking their husbands, and bantering with them about various jobs that would have to be done. "Good thing you can dig a hole" the priest heard one woman say. "We'll need a privy or two out in that field to handle a big crowd." The lady turned to the priest. "Any idea how many to plan on attending?"

Father Jerome looked perplexed. Another problem I didn't think of.

Questions were flowing. The women were excited as they did not get to go to any kind of festivities unless someone was getting married, and then it was only a few select people who were invited. Funerals were well-attended but were not festive.

"We have to involve the children. Please come to me with ideas," spoke Sister Amadeus.

Mary Fields slipped out the side of the open tent. She had started shaking in her knees and arms. Must be all that crowd that got to me. Or, maybe I'm feelin' some bad vibes comin' my way. What will I do? I won't leave Sister Amadeus, that much is for sure. Mary left the service and walked the short path to her cabin. Gotta feed the horses; keep busy and do my job. It's gonna be a long wait 'til I find out. Father Jerome suspects something, too. I saw it on his face when he looked at that homesteader lady. I better tell him that letter I delivered a couple of weeks ago was from her addressed to the Bishop, Diocese of Helena.

When finally, the last of the congregation left the mission yard, the two priests sat together in their humble kitchen both wishing for something stronger than the tea they were drinking.

"Maybe we should go visit Mary. She could put a spring back into our step." The two men looked at their cups. "I'm too tired to make the walk to my bedroom and you can't go visit her alone. That would set up a scandal." Father Michael smiled that behind-the-eyes kind of smile, like he knew a joke but wouldn't say it.

"Yes, I know. I was just wishing out loud. Everything is off to a roaring start, wouldn't you say?" Father Jerome added some sugar to the bitter herb tea.

"Harrumph! We have stirred up a hornet's nest. I have a feeling there is something more behind this visit than attending a party at the fort." The older man stood up slowly, unwinding his feet from the chair legs. "I'm off to my room. Goodnight."

Father Jerome also stood up, but he had to find some boys to help clean up the mess still in the yard. The women had done a good job of clearing off their fancy pies and dishes and silverware that they brought every Sunday for a social after Mass. However he saw this as an opportunity to visit with the young boys.

To serve Mass for the Bishop was a once in a lifetime adventure and privilege. He wanted to build up a desire in their hearts to take an active part in the upcoming events. He walked to the barn and found five youths cleaning stalls, feeding the horse, and rounding up the chickens, housing them for the night. One held a basket; eggs he had collected were overflowing. It was coming on to nightfall; the cow needed milking, along with other chores that had gone unattended during this very surprising day.

Several of the women had decided to take charge before they parted ways Sunday evening. They knew the priests would need more than suggestions. Women from back east, experienced in such matters as planning celebrations would see to it that this *shindig* came off shining a bright light on their part of the territory. The Bishop would expect nothing less. Many of the officers wives from Fort Shaw would be excited to help with the planning; have a chance to wear a fancy frock; show off their jewels. The homesteaders would be happy to attend an event with some *class* to it.

It was about nine o'clock on Monday morning when Father Jerome heard a knock at the mission door. He hurried to open it.

"Well, what can I do for you two so bright and early?" *Leave it to Martha to come to my rescue.*

"Are you decent? We are here to set you straight about this Bishop visit. May we come in?"

He pushed open the screen door and the women stepped into the visiting area.

"Father, we have already made temporary suggestions among ourselves and we would like to ask your permission to just go ahead with the planning of this event. If we know who is coming, *when* they will arrive and *how* many days they plan to visit, everything will work like a well-oiled machine. We can fill in a schedule; bring it to you for approval."

Martha, the leader of the group was skilled at party planning. She had developed Bible studies among the women. Her Altar Society group had seen her steady hand for as long as the Mission had been built, and had even been able to bring in local speakers.

Traveling salesmen showing off their wares, hoping to make enough money to pay for a room at a local boarding house, filled in an afternoon with great entertainment. Most homesteading wives knew it would be years before they would have enough money to buy trivial house-ware items.

"God bless you, Martha. You are the answer to my prayers. Yes, please take charge. I have to get things on the outside in ship-shape as well." He pulled out two of the plain wooden kitchen chairs for the ladies to sit at the table. "Can you whip some men into action, too?"

The ladies laughed. "You just sit back and watch."

When Mary Fields came by after she saw the ladies leave, Father had the letters ready. He had handwritten an invitation to Bear Chief telling him about the celebration. How the Blackfoot Nation responded would be interesting. He hoped no rogue bands would decide to give the Bishop a real whoop-up show. However, he did write that anything they wanted to add to the celebration would be appreciated. Bear Chief could wear his vest and feather bonnet; maybe tell about early days of freedom before reservation living. He also mentioned there would be a baptismal service at the Sun River Crossing. The tribe would have space in the meadow for tipi set ups.

I wonder if he remembers Father Michael and me? We are not those two naïve blackrobes who came up river about the time our government shook things loose for their way of life.

The other letter was an answer to the Bishop's announcement

that he was coming to St. Peter's Mission. Black Mary saw the inked address. She thought seriously of accidentally losing it along the route. *You know you won't do that. You'll take whatever comes to you. You's getting old and fearful.*

T
HE WAGON PULLED into Fort Benton just after noon time. He had forgotten how noisy and busy the fort usually was this time of year. The fur traders were standing in line, all carrying bundles of hides; waiting their turn, visiting with their next-in-line neighbor. The old man put his wagon into an area set aside for wagons; posts were dug into the ground to wrap the horse's reins so they didn't wander off. Mongrel dogs roamed the grounds, some following their owners; others looking for a fight.

The Indian women from various local tribes were inside the building, picking through the beads, material, threads, household dishes and blankets. White women, homesteaders and townsfolk were happy to see the shelves filled with material and goods brought up river that weekend. They worked the counters from the opposite end, hoping to find a few good bargains before everything was sold or traded. A mixture of children checked out the candy bins, making sure the coins they had carefully put into their pants pocket were still there.

The old soldier surveyed the scene. He watched young strong men handling farm equipment: Shovels, axes, nails, hammers, wire, twine; some upset and frowning due to the high prices on the required and necessary products. He slowly walked to the gun counter and picked up a Colt rifle. With reverence he stroked the glossy wood stock and put the rifle to his shoulder testing the balance.

"Can I help you, sir?

"Well. Not right away. I have a list of items to look at and I need oats for my old horse." He turned his head and looked back towards his wagon. "Can you take a look at the furs I brought in today for trade?"

"I can certainly do that, sir. Let's walk out to your wagon and take a look-see at what you brought in today." The young man, dressed in a white starched shirt, wool gray vest and a bolo tie pushed back the sleeves on the shirt. He took time to stretch two large rubber bands on his arms to hold back the material. "I don't want to get my shirt stained. I don't have a laundress to keep clothes clean." The men laughed. "Neither do I. I'm a bachelor; don't see many visitors and so I wear my old clothes every day. Saving the good suit to be buried in one of these days." Again the two shared laughter.

"Have you had any cat hides recently? I've been shooting the big ones that come down by my place back on the river."

"Not the big cats so much. This time of the year we usually see deer, elk, beaver hides. Better trading in the fall, you know." The trader walked briskly to the wagon bed. "We always need beaver hides. Europe and England Royalty like wearing the stove top beaver hats. Your hides probably end up across the ocean on some man's bald head." He chuckled and the old man grinned.

"Yes, but I need some things now, so let's see what you can do for me. I don't recognize you from earlier trips here, but you can bet I only trade at this stop. Old Bent was a fair dealer before he high-tailed it back to Ohio and the States."

"Yes, well, you can be assured the new owners from the fur company in Choteau will be just as fair." He pulled back the rolled up hides. "Let's see what you brought in to us today."

The talk went on for some time until finally a deal for a fair price for two of the hides was reached. He also traded two deer hides and was happy with the dickering.

"Now to get on with why I am here. Here is my list. What can you fill this trip and use the trade money?"

"You are a lucky man. Most everything on your paper here we just unloaded from the boat to the dock. The roustabouts are bringing it up to the warehouse right now."

"Anything else I can do for you?"

"I'm a bit curious about something being planned at St. Peter's Mission in a few weeks. Do you have information about that?"

The clerk looked under the counter to the shelf below. "Here you go. This flyer just came in on the stage with the mail. I haven't had time today to hang it up by the front door yet." He pushed the paper towards the older man. "If you want to take a pencil and write down the date, and why the party, feel free to use my pencil here by the cash register." He pushed the pencil over the counter. "A new barrel of whiskey just came in, too. The plug needs pulling. Help yourself to a drink while I tally up your bill and get you a receipt."

"That's mighty generous of you. I can wet my whistle for sure. It's a long ride in that wagon with no springs on the seat." He looked over the flyer.

"Thank you. I was the commander of Ft. Shaw when it was being built. This would be a nice celebration for me to attend. Might be some of my old Army buddies there, too."

He took the pencil and tore a corner off the flyer to write the necessary information. When he finished, he folded the paper and stuffed it into his vest pocket. "I wonder if they sent this flyer up to Browning to the reservation." He thought a minute. "Probably did. "It was way before your time. My soldiers pushed the whole village into the Glacier country to land reserved for them to live on. They had their village right over there on the other side of the river and were moved about the time the Mission priests came up river."

He emptied his glass and pushed himself away from the counter. "Yes, sir. This just might be something for me to think about." He picked up the handwritten receipt off the counter and folded that paper, stuffing it into the same vest pocket as the information about the anniversary celebration planned at St. Peter's Mission.

"Thanks again for your trading with me. You did a fair deal. I'll be back looking for you come fall; or when I run out of flour." He chuckled to himself at his attempt to say something funny. The horse stood head down, waiting patiently to begin the trek back home.

He raised his tattered straw hat into the air. Some men jumped out of the horse's path allowing the old man access to leave through the open log gate. The wagon jolted every time it hit a rut or rock on the road. The dog had jumped onto the tail end, tired at the end of this busy day. The old man, lost in memories but excited about the Fort Shaw shindig, hung on to the reins. He let out his usual yell reversing the words when the cave entrance came into view.

"Yahoo! Here we come."

26

F LOWER WOMAN RODE behind Bear Chief's horse. She was ready to make the trip back to the Village and to see her children. They would have many questions for her. One question Bear Chief finally answered was that he planned to call a meeting of the sub-chiefs and announce his decision about attending the St. Peter's Mission celebration. He would have to clear it with the Indian Agent whose office was in the town of Browning.

Those who wanted to leave the reservation and go back to the Mission area would be under the watchful eyes of many warriors. They would caravan together since the younger natives, reservation born, would not know the hidden trails that would make the trip much shorter.

Flower woman was happy. I want to stop and visit the grave of my still born baby one more time. Many of my family will be at the Mission. Looking Back needs a change. She and I can keep track of the children on the trail. We will have Wise Owl and Little Bear to help set up two small tipis; travois loaded with food and other necessities.

She looked at Bear Chief's back once again. He is not sitting straight. Should I stop him? I wonder what is bothering him with pain. She studied his back looking for clues. No, I'll not confront him just yet. This can wait. I'll mention it to our Medicine Man in a day or two if he seems out of sorts. They rode on in silence, each deep in their own thoughts.

"Bear Chief. Stop. We need water. There is no hurry. Listen to me. I need a break from this fast pace you have set us on."

Bear Chief looked over his shoulder, but he did not halt his horse.

"We will stop at Duck Lake."

This alarmed Flower Woman; something was not right. *Maybe Eagle Feather can find out what ails him.* She continued to follow her Chief and said nothing more.

It was a beautiful morning with promise of a hot afternoon. Bear Chief wanted to make it back to the Village while his horse still carried his head high. This would be an important return for Bear Chief.

His vision stayed with him long after the bear had left his camp on top of the mountain. He needed to pray with elders; ask for guidance about the future of his tribe. He had not been feeling quite like himself for several moons now but said nothing to Flower Woman. Things were rapidly changing in his world; he saw himself aging, less strength in his muscled arms and legs; eating much less meat, tired before his usual day's end.

As he led the way, his mind wandered. Memories of his youth, his achievements for bravery, leadership, came as if a damn had burst, flooding his very soul. I'm getting old. This is too soon for me to give up my way of life. The Great Spirit sent me many messages on the mountain. I'll not tell Flower Woman of my concerns. I'll lead all who want to return to our old homeland for the celebration, but it will be a humbling experience for me. I am disappointed that she does not see the push from the Army as defeat for me. As the horse cantered at a comfortable pace, the crude leather saddle that this warrior had sat upon his whole life, created its own sounds, a rhythm Bear Chief loved to hear. It seemed to sing to him that he was the leader of a great Nation of the People. I will give Little Bear this saddle. The rifle I've held in my hands for more seasons than I can count? I'll not pull the trigger again but Wise Owl will; my bow and arrows I'll give to Wise Owl. He will protect Flower Woman and Looking Back and the family for years to come. My shaking hands that I've kept secret for many moons will sign one more paper written by Eagle Feather. He will keep my secrets for many more seasons, but I plan to take care of this give-away while I am still strong and before I am replaced.

"Bear Chief." He thought he heard someone call his name. Yes. It was a familiar voice bringing him back to the present. Flower Woman rode up alongside his horse. "My back and legs need to move on the ground. Stop now. We are at the shore of Duck Lake."

Her voice did not betray her thoughts. She was steady in her words, even though she had fear in her heart as she watched Bear Chief sitting askew in his saddle. He has something bothering him. I must be patient. He will tell me in his time. My great warrior, lover and friend must have seen something in his vision. He will try to remain in control for as long as he can. He is too proud to give in to this loop of his life that he is entering. Old age comes too soon.

The water in the leather bag stayed cool and it refreshed them as they watched the birds on Duck Lake. Flower Woman walked the shores; picked up small stones that spoke to her.

Bear Chief drank the healing herb tea and ate some sourdough bread. He was much stronger now and the brain fog had cleared.

"Come woman. It isn't much further to our reservation." Bear Chief held the reins for both horses and waited for Flower Woman to mount. Then, as if showing off in front of her, Bear Chief leaped into the air landing with his palms on the rump of the animal. His powerful arms lifting his body over the horse's back, making a perfect summer salt. He slipped his moccasins easily into the stirrups, pulled back the reins, wrenching the animal's neck into a high arc. The beautiful stallion reared up, hit the ground, reared again and man and beast became one as they galloped across the meadow.

Flower Woman felt joy return to her heart. Her Bear Chief was back in mind and spirit, even if the body showed signs of pain.

The nearer they came to the reservation fence, both animals picked up their pace at the first smell of wood smoke. They dreamed their own dream; a bucket of oats would be waiting for them.

Wise Owl stood by the corral gate, waiting patiently for their return. The whole village suspected something big was going to happen when Bear Chief and Flower Woman left for a vision quest. They were gone for four days. Wise Owl had kept guard at the gate, fasting and sleeping. He waved his arm extended high over his head. Bear Chief spotted the flash of movement and color from the huge red flag.

"Look at our welcome home warrior. He has a bow and arrow posed as if to shoot into the sky." Bear Chief laughed and Flower Woman waved. Her horse whinnied.

"Bear Chief. Wise Owl truly loves you and respects you. You must bring him into the circle of your protector warriors."

"Ho-ka-hay! Wise Owl grabbed the reins tossed over to him. The couple slid to the ground, happy to be home. Flower Woman walked up the path to her tipi. She suppressed a giggle bubbling up inside her. There stood Looking Back and all the children standing in a circle waiting to welcome them home. Peace and love filled her heart and tears gathered in the corners of her eyes. "How wonderful to see you all behaving so nicely." She teased. "I need to leave more often." The children looked toward Looking Back. She raised her right arm and they started singing a welcome song; the smaller children falling onto the grass and rolling with laughter.

Elders, as if on que, came to the front of the tipi. "Welcome home, great Chief. We heard rumors; news from Eagle Feather and your runners.

Bear Chief sighed. He had hoped to sleep before meeting with this group.

"Listen to your Chief." He paused. "Meet me in the large tipi. We have many things to discuss. I want to say it only once so send a messenger to the men who are not here now. Then I will begin." *I need to help Flower woman empty our parfleche. Little Bear can help with that. Where is Eagle Feather? I want to smoke a pipe with him first about the vision I received.*

The crowd disbanded. A few women went to their tipis to bring back food as was their tradition. Youngsters were sent to gather firewood and stack it near the tipi in case the meeting stretched into the late night when the cold winds would blow.

Soon it felt festive. Their chief was back with news from the Great Spirit; fire pits were ready to heat stew and coffee, and the night winds were mellow, carrying smoke through the branches of the pine trees. Soon stars would fill the cloudless sky.

Bear Chief turned to Little Bear. "Son, go find Eagle Feather. Tell him to bring pencil and paper; that he is to sit next to me on my right side. I want this meeting recorded. Also, I want him to speak to the gathered about what he heard from the white-man's tongue."

"Yes, Father." Little Bear took off running to find Eagle Feather. He frowned as he ran. Something is not right with Bear Chief. I will take better watch over him now that I am aware.

He found his friend. "Bear Chief is back. He wants you to come to him for a smoke."

Eagle Feather dropped the knife he was working on, trying to cut a deer horn to the right size to be a handle for the blade. "Return to him, Little Bear. I will be there soon."

"Wise Owl and I are to sit to your right."

Eagle Feather raised his eye brows as if surprised. Something big was about to be revealed. "Get along, now. I'll come in full ceremonial dress."

Flower Woman yawned and rubbed her eyes. The last week had been long and difficult; full of mystery. Her instincts told her a new way of life would soon descend upon their village. *I'll ask Looking Back to keep watch on Bear Chief to see if he is in pain.* She would make teas for him from the many concoctions she had collected over the years. She was proud to be his wife. His leadership for so many seasons had kept their village alive despite government controls and their rules over the Blackfoot Nation.

She heard the drums. The time for her to go to the big tipi was now. She would sit outside the flap waiting for orders. She would do her part as Bear Chief's wife seeing that tobacco filled the pipes; that food was plentiful when needed.

Children were at home being watched by teenaged siblings. A few babies slept in their woven baskets, or cradle boards, covered with warm blankets to keep the night flies away.

Men greeted each other in the traditional way. They filed into the tipi in sacred order according to their status with the tribal council. A silence permeated the space and the fire flamed casting shadows on the tipi walls. The flames cast off enough warmth to hold back the cool air coming into the tipi as darkness overcame the outside world.

Bear Chief began the ceremony. He held the ceremonial pipe with both hands, then he pointed it to the north. A prayer was said by an elder. The pipe pointed to the south and another prayer rose out of the silence from a sub-chief on the south side of the tent. This ritual was repeated with the pipe pointing the west and then to the east.

Little Bear and Wise Owl had never been allowed to attend this sacred ritual and it was like Bear Chief was casting a magic spell over the group. He then struck the earth offering a prayer to Mother Earth. Father Sky was the sixth part of the ritual. When a silence once again came over the room Bear Chief thrust the pipe straight up to the Great Spirit. Little Bear jumped at the suddenness of the action.

Wise Owl and Little Bear each held the pipe and took a small puff, choking as they did so. Neither boy had tried smoking until that night. Finally, the pipe made the complete circle and Bear Chief placed it on a sacred stand made just for the pipe. He never wanted the pipe to fall, or crack as this was a special gift from Eagle Feather with much meaning behind its being made.

Bear Chief began speaking. "Welcome. Five days ago Flower Woman and I left the reservation, against government rules and rode horses to Chief Mountain. I climbed the trail and fasted for three days on the top praying to my Great Spirit. My spirit guide blessed me by staying with me the whole time. Flower Woman stayed at the base of the mountain praying for a successful spiritual time for me." He looked across the tipi floor and watched the shadows on the tipi wall.

"The first night I set up my rug and directional flags. It was a warm night and the stars seemed to cover me with bright lights. I did not sleep and I fasted without any problems. My bear stayed by my side. I did drift off into a fog the second night and my bear nudged me many times to keep me awake so I could hear the message when it came." The young boys took in every word. They knew very little about Vision Quests at their young ages.

"Listen to your Chief." Bear Chief took a deep breath.

"I asked if we should take part in the St. Peter's Mission anniversary party. The Great Spirit said yes; with government permission. Any who want to attend should do so. We are to stay together. Young braves born after the big push know nothing about our village life back then. We suffered great humiliation and despair but we obeyed and did not fight the soldiers. I knew we could not win. A few renegade braves caused some trouble for a while, but they, too, realized it was frustration that would not change.

Those who attend are to teach their children about what the soldiers did protecting the homesteaders. They will see our cemeteries in decay, and Mother Earth plowed into furrows. We were called savages and children who could not care for ourselves in the changing white man world.

"Listen to your chief. We will take our own food and small tipis. We will camp together in the meadow behind the Mission. We will not cause any harm by fighting or stealing. Do you hear me? Understand what I am saying? We will show them we have learned their ways. We will be 'civilized'. Some of the older men cackled while others choked up a bit. "We'll try, Chief. But you are asking way too much of us. The rendezvous mountain men will have all the fun." Laughter broke out and the women eavesdropping giggled at what they heard.

Looking Back whispered to Flower Woman. "We can get the travois ready with short poles for two tipis. I have mixed feelings, too. The cemetery where my husband lies will not be easy to pass by, nor will it be for you."

Bear Chief spoke again. "The white man's blackrobe is called a Bishop. He is coming to the Mission and he is the one who will be honored. He has never seen the Mission. There will be baptisms at Sun River Crossing. You are all free to partake if you want to. The Christian Mass will be said daily. Weddings will be open to the public. The fort ladies want to have a fancy dinner and dance night."

Eagle Feather spoke up. "Many of you elders will remember the two blackrobes who came up river driving the squeaky two-wheeled cart." He laughed. "I remember their horse would have ended up in our stew pot." He went to the flap and opened it. Flower Woman stood on the other side with a huge wooden spoon in her hand. "We have stew. Anyone who is hungry, come out now."

Bear Chief, Eagle Feather and the two young boys eagerly lead the procession to the cooking pots hanging over the fire pits on iron stakes.

EVERYTHING THAT COULD be thought of was listed in the plans for the celebration, stretching into the second week of activities. Father Jerome had way too many irons in the fire.

Happy to be receiving responses from people in near-by towns as well as the local Catholic population that he had sent out handwritten invitations; word of mouth was faster. The anniversary of the fort reminded the valley homesteaders of the comfort and security it provided them. Every knock on the Mission door revealed more volunteers.

The town of Ft. Shaw benefited as well. Men took on roles of leadership: Sheriff, town mayor and carpenters. Woman schoolmarms and laundresses; dressmakers and café owners and book keepers for the mercantile stores offered their potluck foods and desserts. No one was turned away who had offered to help; Indians and riff-raff travellers as well.

Martha and her planning committee had no problems finding help. Volunteers from Fort Shaw brought creative back-east ideas. The men would be needed to hang decorations, mark off spaces for the buggies and wagons; build a pole corral to keep horses, mules and donkeys confined in one part of the Mission field. Her bubbling spirit was infectious. The owner of the lumber mill offered two men and supplies for a grandstand.

"This is history in the making," she'd say as she started every meeting with a prayer for the success of their venture. Her biggest worry was the weather. Even Martha could not control the clouds and the chance of rain. Whenever Father Michael saw Martha coming up the path he'd retreat to his room, leaving the whole program to Father Jerome.

Harrumph! All this fall-da-rah. I wonder what the Bishop really wants. Certainly something more than a fancy party.

Down the road a few miles the old man decided he'd go to the party. He'd ride his horse and take his dog. He would sleep in the barracks like in the old days. *Best dig out that old trunk and see what I can salvage to wear that is half-decent and still fits.*

The old man stretched his aching body to reach the leather trunk stored on the back shelf and pulled on the strap handles, freeing it from years of neglect. He set it on the edge of his bed, released the latches and lifted the top. Stored all these years, the Union Officer's blue coat and button shirt and pants; uniform, plumed feather hat, gloves and sword look none the worse for wear. *I wonder if I can still fit into this fancy parade outfit. I want to wear it to the anniversary party next week.* He stroked his facial beard. *I haven't shaved in years. Don't think I will now, either. I could trim my hair back but the curls make me look like General George Armstrong Custer.* He held the jacket up to his chest. Not owning a mirror, he could only guess how it looked. In his memory he pictured himself; young, strong and handsome. He was proud of his Army years, starting as a private and retiring from the fort as the commander in charge. That was a sad-happy time, but he was glad he'd mustered out when he did.

He returned to the trunk to see what other surprises were there to stir up his past. A flag from the men at the fort was rolled up. He brought it out of the trunk; gave it a hearty shake. *I'll hang that on a pole outside for folks traipsing by on that upper trail.* A folder stuffed with discharge papers and a couple of forgotten books cluttered the bottom. *Huh! I wondered where that book was.* The Holy Bible. *That should be on the table by the lamp.*

Something bright yellow and orange caught his eye. He grabbed it and brought out the large square of torn calico material. *What? What is this?* Then it hit him hard. *That material belonged to my dear wife.* It was the only reminder of her. He carefully pressed the cloth open with his gnarled hands; then he lost control. Tears streamed down his face and mixed into his gray-black beard.

"Where are you? Where is our son?" He screamed the words as he slumped onto a chair stump. His voice ricocheted inside the cave. "Why do I never get an answer?

He stood up; legs wobbly. The yellow material he put with the uniform. *I'll wear a yellow scarf in memory of you.*

The dog is making quite a racket. Someone must be coming. He used his shirt sleeve to wipe his face and walked to the edge of the path. His dog growled low in his throat and hair stood up on his back behind his head. "Hush. Be quiet." He heard scraping sounds from the travois poles. Small rocks slipped over the edge of the trail and landed near his corral.

A band of Indians was moving toward the Fort. *Must be headed for the anniversary party.* One young boy, maybe fifteen years old or so, was gawking over the trail edge, trying to find the entrance into the cave dweller's place. Their eyes made contact. Neither spoke and the procession moved on. Another young brave, maybe in his twenties, was keeping the family together. Two women brought up the end of the group, walking ponies loaded down with tent poles. They were unaware of his presence, or maybe they didn't care that he was so near. They seemed more interested in their surroundings and were chatting in Blackfoot as they fell behind the little children.

I wonder if Bear Chief and his band will attend. What we did to him was harsh. Now I can see how unfair it was to move them out of their homeland. He shrugged and returned to the entrance of his cave. *Best be feeding the horse and myself before it gets to be nightfall.* His eyes fell on the items he had left on his bed. He pulled the trunk out of the way and found an empty hook to hang the pants and coat so they could air out. He put on his garden hat to go take care of the evening chores. He had to lock up his chickens and make sure the wire gate was hooked. Coyotes liked chicken as much as he did. He went about his evening chores. *Do I really want to go to that anniversary party? Can I do it? I'll have to think about the memories before I decide. What's in it for me?* He picked up the Holy Bible and caressed the book cover. *Is there a hidden message for me in this book? Maybe it would be good for me to have a visit with the blackrobes if they could find a bit of time to see me.* He put the book down on the little circle of a table top. His dog danced around the cave entrance. He picked up his metal bowl with his sharp teeth and dropped it at his master's feet.

❖ ❖ ❖ ❖ ❖

28

EVERYTHING LOOKED FRESH and inviting around the Mission. The priests were ready for their guest. Wagons full of locals lined the road. They were excited to hear the roar of the big cannon, alerting everyone for miles around that the Bishop's black coach, like a fancy stage coach, had topped the knoll in the hill.

Flags flapped in the ever present wind; a soldier stood at attention along the roadside, guarding the Bishop's cortege as it approached the crossroads. A viewing stand had been built in the front yard of the Mission House and the dignitaries were seated. A military band placed their instruments carefully across their knees, waiting for the signal to begin.

"Hooray! Here they come! Look. Look everybody. Look!" The youngster, dressed in his best Sunday-go-to-meeting clothes started jumping up and down on the roof of the house. He pointed off to his right, waving his Irish cap to catch the driver's attention. "Turn here!"

His mother almost fainted when she saw her son up so high acting like a sentinel. "Johnnie! You come down here this instant." She waved her arms at the boy, but he pretended not to see or hear her.

The crowd started to clap and wave. Some, in their excitement, whistled so loud it hurt ears on people standing close. The driver snapped his long, fancy black horse whip into an overhead figure eight; almost losing his black top hat He stepped on a brake pedal that made a fluttering sound. The Bishop had rolled down the curtained windows and smiled and waved back at the people. The horses slowed in time to turn into the open gate. The well-groomed creatures were used to this kind of attention. They slowed to a stop. Children ran up to pet the beautiful, shining black hide, taking no heed to mothers warning their children to back away and give the animals space.

Little Bear, Wise Owl, Flower Woman, Looking Back, and the children gaped at the unfolding performance. They had arrived the day before and set up their tipi. With a front row view they watched how the white man welcomed this Bishop. Only Flower Woman knew a few white man words, but her family recognized waving hand signals and laughter. She felt captivated by the women who linked elbows to form a path for the man wearing black robes; almost afraid when she was pulled into the line. Little Bear moved to rescue her. Wise Owl stopped him, pushing Looking Back into the line next to Flower Woman. "We are here to participate, aren't we?"

A little blonde girl, about 5 years old, carried a huge bouquet of wild flowers to give to the Bishop. He accepted her gift, thanking her with a pat on her head. He reached into his pocket to find a holy card with a picture of Jesus for her to stick in the edge of her dresser mirror frame. She beamed up at him, smiling from ear to ear.

"I'll keep this card forever." Her voice sounded like a little bird trilling. Off she ran to show everyone her special prize.

Indian drummers sat with their padded sticks, circled in the yard. At the sight of the blackrobe they began a sacred song to the Great Spirit. Little Bear noticed the crowd settle into a calmer attitude; peaceful, instead of the frenzy he witnessed at first. *Our drums have power. White man is hearing it, feeling it.*

The Bishop walked to the stand and took the megaphone in hand. He thanked the crowd for attending, surprised at what had been done to bring him into their world. He let his eyes wander over the heads and hats of the men and women standing before him. He searched until he found what he was looking for. *Ah. There she is; way in the back as if she is about to bolt. I must speak to Father Jerome about her when we have a quiet moment. I'm to be here for several days. There will be time to do what I have come to do.*

As if she had been struck by a bolt of lightning, Black Mary stepped outside of the crowd. Instinctively, she felt his stare.

Little Bear followed the line of the bishop's eyes. That woman has black skin. She is darker than any of us. I've never seen someone colored like her before. Is she American? Indian? Where does she live? As soon as I see my father, I must find out these answers. What is there for me to learn besides our tribe's way of life? Surely it is time for answers. I am not a child any more. Little Bear felt a strange stirring in his heart and soul and head.

Suddenly he was pushed toward the food tables. "Come on. Let's go eat white man's food while it is still there," shouted Wise Owl. He had several of his brothers and sisters in tow. "Looking Back is helping at the end of the line. Can you imagine one of us working side by side with a white woman?" Both young men laughed as they made their way to the tables.

Wise Owl seemed unaware of the many stares their way. Not many of the farm children had ever had contact with a Blackfoot Indian, dressed in hides with elk teeth beaded across their shirts, and wore hide shoes. In their world Indian people purchased Levi jeans, canvas tents, and farm equipment. Women made men's shirts and their dresses from material sent up river from St. Louis. Leather high-button shoes lasted as hand-me-downs for several children in one family.

Pushing the Blackfoot Nation high into the Backbone country for reservation-born members did not hold the same memories as it did for the elders of the tribe, like Bear Chief and Eagle Feather. Every one there came for personal reasons, reliving their past, or questioning how it used to be for pioneers who made good farms out of toil and strength and perseverance.

Little Bear watched it all in disbelief. He now understood why Bear Chief did not want to return. He had listened to old-timers from the fort laughing and reminiscing about the Indian wars. With each story Little Bear felt confused and resentful. *I wonder what Wise Owl thinks? These soldiers were not respectful of the Nation's traditions; they stole our land and our dignity.*

Suddenly, Little Bear was not hungry. He tasted bile in his mouth as he bolted from the line and ran back to their tipi. *No one is going to humble me. I am not a savage from a Wild West show.* Little Bear dropped on top of his sleeping robes. *Great Spirit you know why we are here. Tell me.* He doubled up his fists and struck the fur hide; blow after blow.

Flower Woman had no idea that trouble was to come from the North for Little Bear. This rendezvous would become the first of many occasions for Little Bear to glimpse the racial hatred that existed between the Indian and the Whites. Living on the reservation shielded him in many ways from the reality of the world on the other side of the fence.

29

D ARKNESS DESCENDED FORCING parents to load their children into the wagons for their trip home, with promises they would return the next day. Waves and hoots of laughter could be heard from each wagon load when it passed through the open gate.

"See you in the morning, Martha. Try and get some sleep, if you can." Shouted Elizabeth, her friend and helper. The women waved to each other.

"Will try; no promises." Her smiling face did not betray her very tired eyes. Her back was screaming with pain and she wanted nothing more than to sit down. Father Jerome pulled out a kitchen chair for her and handed her a cup of chamomile tea.

"Well, Martha. You pulled it off. What a great welcome for the Bishop." He sipped the hot liquid and sighed. "You best be getting home. Tomorrow will be a long one."

Martha emptied the cup and handed the good priest a schedule for the next day's events.

It would begin at 11:00 A.M. with a church service. The bishop was to receive a stole handmade of the finest hide and decorated with colorful beads in a typical Blackfoot design, white, black and red being the dominant colors.

When the bead-woman presented it to Father Jerome for his approval he could only stare at the beautiful piece of art work. *The Bishop will treasure this.* The scene was of a mountain peak covered with snow, blended in with pine tree tops pointing to heaven. Next came a flowing river and next to it was a magnificent bead-decorated tipi;

poles intersecting in a perfect circle of yellow beads. A gray swirl like smoke lifted from the tipi hole. As if to say "Welcome" the door flap was open. A sturdy pole next to the tipi held a feathered chieftain's bonnet.

When the bead-woman saw the delight in Father Jerome's face she picked up the stole and put it around his shoulders. "I make you one like it when we have a party for you."

Father Jerome carefully removed the garment from his black robe and placed it carefully on the kitchen table. He brushed at his eyes. I wonder if she has had a prediction about me from her Great Spirit. Not now, Lord. Please, not now. I don't want to just be the seed planter. I want to bring in the harvest. I won't need a party for many more years, God willing. He heard Martha calling his name. He came back to the moment and slapped the table top.

"Time is ticking away, and we both need rest." He walked her to the door. Her buggy and horse stood waiting for her. "Good night, Father. Tomorrow will be a wonderful day full of preaching for you two priests. You will have many in line to sign up to be baptized Saturday at the Sun River Crossing. Oh! Before I forget to tell you, the great and honored Blackfoot leader, Bear Chief, is to arrive late in the afternoon."

"Good night, Martha. Plenty of time to fill me in tomorrow." He chuckled softly. *What a woman that one is. She never runs out of things to say.*

He picked up the lantern and headed for the back door. "Please dear Lord, light my path and have my hay-bed covered with soft buffalo robes." He rubbed his forehead. *I can't complain. Jesus slept where he could. He didn't even have a rock on which to lay his head.*

B ear Chief and Eagle Feather smoked a pipe offering prayers of thankfulness for their health; asked for protection over the village and protection for the members who had left for the St. Peter's Mission celebration. Both men were quiet, deep into their own thoughts about their leaving for the trip back to their old land. Finally, Eagle Feather broke the silence.

"Do you have people in place to care for the horses; to keep check on the reservation?" "Yes." Bear Chief spoke hesitantly. He still had misgivings about attending.

"Flower Woman, Looking Back, the children, left two moons ago. Runners have brought me messages that they are safe. Tipis fill the meadow once again near the Sun River." He took one last pull on the sacred pipe and handed it to Eagle Feather. "Do not relight the pipe, Eagle Feather. We must leave now."

"I am ready. My eagle feather will be stuck into my long braids and I have a white man's shirt, vest, and pants in a parfleche; I will toss it on to a travois." He glanced at Bear Chief.

"Tomorrow I will ride as naked as I dare…and bareback; my pinto painted on his shoulders. He will have a few long ribbons woven into his mane and tail. We will prance together and I will yell a few blood-curdling war whoops when we reach the gate." He laughed. I haven't done that for how many years now?"

Bear Chief stood up. "You will scare the wits out of them." His eyes twinkled at the idea.

"I have to wear a chest plate covered in elk teeth, weighing more than my body should have to carry." He looked around the tipi. "Flower Woman packed and took my war bonnet. It will be expected of me to wear that in the parade. She will be dressed in her royal leather dress with all the fringe and jingle bells." He laughed. "Maybe this will turn out to be a grand time for our people to see how we used to be; not so many years ago." He sighed. "What was so good about the good old days?" He lifted sorrowful eyes.

Eagle Feather lifted the flap. Our horses are outside. Many families wait to move out with us."

Bear Chief walked outside and was surprised. He spoke to the gathered few.

"Many of you do not know the way back. Stay together. We are ready now. I give you my blessing." Bear Chief raised his hands, palm down, and faced toward the gathered peoples. "May you be protected on the journey, be healthy. Be peaceful and use this trip back into time as a teaching for your children. Talk to them about everything they see and ask you about. Send them to me if you need help."

With that, Eagle Feather and Bear Chief mounted their horses and started the exodus.

F ORT SHAW FROM the exterior looked like a solid protection of rock walls; buildings and corrals for the horses. Several rock houses lined the left side of the roadway leading in to the fort. The houses, built from mud squares, supplied proper amenities for officers and their wives; decorated in the style of the day. Kentucky Blue Grass seed, planted with great care, thrived in sparse patches. Women valiantly planted cottonwood seedlings; trees uprooted from the edge of the river, hoping the wagon wheel rim placed around the base would catch water. Grown trees meant shade.

Army wives came west, following their soldier husbands. Most only stayed a few weeks finding life too difficult for them to accept.

Others intended to stay permanently. Their reward would be a few acres for the time spent fighting the Indians. Soldiers saw this as a carrot held out in front of their noses; not quite able to grasp it, but trying their best to win the prize. Three months in the Army seemed too good to be true. The single soldier, when his tour was up, drifted further west to find gold; not intending to return east to poverty; or to plagues like the Cholera that persisted in largely populated areas.

Several structures on the fort grounds, made from cottonwood logs, housed servants, a laundry, and a bakery. A hospital, staffed with a medical doctor and a nurse, was one of the first buildings completed. When the fort was first occupied tents housed the soldiers. Cooks made do in a mess tent.

As the mud from the river was turned into stone blocks, buildings gave a fortified look to fences. This fort was an artillery base. Cannons, other large weapons lined in rows, were stored. Most had not been used for many years since the Indian Peace Treaties were being honored by both sides.

The fort commander looked over the landscape. *So much has been done under my watch. I won't miss this place, however, when I finally get a promotion that I think is long overdue. I like the comforts of city life, I readily admit.* He waited patiently for the Bishop's coach to arrive. A platform had been built for the dignitaries that were already driving through the fort gate.

The women had an early supper planned in the new dining room-kitchen. Red-white-blue bunting was draped across the front portion of the stage. The fort's insignia, painted on a large piece of canvas, could be seen from anywhere in the hall. The band looked sharp in their parade dress uniforms. They wanted to show off their musical skills and long hours of practice filled their evenings after completing their daily assignments. Most of the musical instruments were battered bugles, accordions, whistles and an out of tune piano.

All-in-all, with the sunshine promising a clear day, army cooks and waiters prepared a splendid meal. Hot apple pie, still baking in the field ovens, would top off the meal.

"No one will leave here hungry," said a private as he made gallons of coffee.

"Where do you suppose the Commander found grapes?"

The aroma of coffee filled the kitchen; sliced potatoes sizzled on the top burners, along with sausage from the fort-raised pigs. Hundreds of bakery rolls crowded tin plates; fresh butter and real cream pitchers were placed in the center of each table.

"All we need now is the guest of honor," spoke one of the waiters when he poked his head outside for some cooler air.

The excited artillery guards at the gate spotted the coach as sunlight flashed across the brass bar connected to the tongue. The canon, already loaded, only needed a Lucifer stick tossed into its holder. Standing at attention, saluting the big gun, the Corporal struck the stick. In less than one could count to ten the ball shot out the barrel; the roar to be heard for miles. Early arrivals with children in their wagons lined the roadway. Young boys watched in awe; girls covered their ears and cried.

Soldiers immediately stood at attention and watched as the fancy coach passed on by.

The Commander stood at the end of the graveled path. He waited for his aid to open the coach door to escort the Bishop. "Welcome to Fort Shaw your eminence."

Would you look at that man? His black robes, cape and top hat? He's outdone himself among all of us in our parade blues. Well, for the parade I'll wear my plumed hat and my dress suit and presentation sword. We will be in competition for the best dressed man at this festivity.

"Thank you. I had no idea the size and scope of your fort. You must run it with an iron fist."

"You are quite right. Every man here knows his place. We have a stockade, but seldom is it used. It is peace time, thank God. The Indians are adapting to this new way of life." He smiled. "Oh, you probably hear about a few renegade bands in the area."

"Yes. I read Ned Buntline stories when they are available."

"Believe about half of those stories and you will be more informed as to what is really happening here in the west. We have growth, statehood, civilization." He raised his hand and pointed toward the many buildings. "Twenty years ago there was nothing here. Now we provide protection for most of the western territories."

"Churches of all denominations are coming into this land, also." The Bishop smiled. "That means a mission field for our priests; families grow towns; businesses keep it all together."

Just then a Corporal approached the two men. He saluted the Commander.

"The meal is about to be served sir. We want to seat our guest first. If you will follow me please." He clicked his very shiny boot heels as he turned toward the kitchen; Bishop and Commander following directly behind him.

After the commotion of soldiers entering the space, the commander stood up and shook a brass bell that was placed by a waiter on the right side of the plate.

"Attention." He paused for a moment then shook the bell again, this time louder. A quiet filled the room. "It is my pleasure to welcome this morning…His Excellency." The Bishop waved.

Some of the soldiers stood up, a few cheered and others clapped.

"Bishop, would you say a few words?"

"Yes, of course. I'll say more than a few probably. I usually do."

The Bishop stood tall with folded hands and closed eyes.

"Dear Lord, thank you for bringing me to this fort. Keep everyone safe. I ask a blessing for the hands that prepared this food. Now let's eat." He reached down and picked up his coffee mug. The mess hall burst into laughter and hands clapped. Some soldiers returned the salute to the Bishop with their cup.

The commander waved to the cooks to bring on the platters full of food. Waiters walked among the tables pouring water and more coffee. Some awed and oohed. A voice shouted, "When are you coming back again, Bishop? We don't get to eat like this every day."

After the meal the commander took the Bishop on a tour of the grounds.

"Impressive." He walked over to inspect the cannons. They were from the Civil War era.

"We are ready for most anything that comes along."

The commander noticed a group of older men standing by the gate. "Let's walk over to that group and see what they are up to."

They approached the older men, dressed in their ill-fitting uniforms from their past duty at the fort.

"Good afternoon, gentlemen. What can I help you with?"

"Nothin. We's waitin' to see the Bishop."

"Here I am. Will you be attending services when the sun cools this afternoon?"

"If'n we ain't found us a tree to take a nap under."

The Bishop laughed. "I'd like to join you for that nap. However, should your plans change; I'll be at the Mission just down the road a few miles."

Another man spoke up. "I'm here wantin' to see Bear Chief of the

Blackfoot Nation. I always held him in great respect. He kept his village runnin' like a handwoun' clock."

"The Chief is expected to arrive later today. He and his entourage will enter into St. Peter's Mission probably at dusk."

"Thanks for that information." The gray-haired man who had faithfully served in the Union Army at Fort Shaw many years ago stood at attention and saluted the commander.

The salute passed from soldier to soldier.

"Pleased to visit with you, sir. What ever happened to the commander when we was serving probably 20 years ago?"

"Good you should remember. I'll ask if anyone knows where he is. Word will get back to you. If he is present we'll see to it you have a reunion."

The Bishop's coach and horses stood waiting for him to enter. He had a schedule to keep; people waited for him back at the Mission. Dust billowed up behind the coach as it left the gate.

⸻◆◆◆⸻

32

T HE TRAVOIS MOVED at a steady pace. Eagle Feather and Bear Chief alternated between leading them and bringing up the stragglers. Once a familiar scene came into view the elders would stop and stare. Many said prayers for release of grief to their Great Spirit when they saw their sacred burial grounds. The small tree had grown and hid his son's mound.

Bear Chief stopped his horse. His emotions still ran high for his stillborn baby boy. Is that a bear in the bushes? Yes, he did see the shining eyes of a black bear lying next to the mound. Aah. So you are still protecting my son, are you? Thank you spirit guide for showing yourself to me today. It is a comfort knowing you are always near when I need your guidance; your help in decisions that are sometimes very hard to make.

Eagle Feather watched Bear Chief stop his horse at the mound. He kept the group moving as best he could. Once past that familiar spot, the rest of the trail would be easy for the travelers; harder to keep them together.

Each travois carried provisions for the people and for the dogs and ponies pulling the loads. No one had on special clothes. They were saving them for the morning and the parade from St. Peter's Mission down the road to the Sun River's Crossing.

Many of the tribal members were anxious to meet the Bishop and be baptized by such a holy man of the white man's God. Bear Chief did not object to anyone being baptized and thence-forth be called a Christian. His family had all been baptized several years ago when a

Jesuit missionary group came to the reservation. For himself, he was content with his faith in his Great Spirit; his spirit guides and family.

The fort finally came into view; tipi smoke curled high into the air alerting the travelers that they were late arriving. At the top of the rise, Eagle Feather and Bear Chief halted the procession.

"You are now to go through the gate at St. Peter's mission. You, who understand the white man's tongue, ask where to set up camp." He looked at Eagle Feather.

"You come with me. We will sneak in by a back way. Our tipis will have signals; Flower Woman will have cots and food for us." He nudged his horse forward. "Where did you jump that fence when I sent you here years ago?"

Eagle Feather looked over the area. "It is all changed now. Much growth since I here last." He slapped his reins against the horse's neck. He stayed alongside Bear Chief as they rode swiftly through the tall meadow grasses. "You are in big trouble with Flower Woman, Chief. It's dark; the moon is not out." He laughed.

Bear Chief pretended not to hear him. He knew he was late. "I'm the chief over everything, even Flower Woman." He closed in his fingers on his right hand, crossed his chest and hit is heart two times.

Eagle Feather almost fell off his horse laughing so hard at what Bear Chief had just proclaimed. You are her slave and have been since the first time you laid your eyes on her. She has captivated you and you don't even know it.

Bear Chief watched for a signal as to how to find their tipi. He didn't expect Little Bear to be standing alone in the grasses, waiting for him.

"Over here, my father. Flower Woman has everything ready for you. Eagle Feather will stay in our tipi also." Little Bear's voice was flat, angry almost. Bear Chief immediately heard the sadness, or confusion, in the young man's tone and actions.

"Grab my reins, Little Bear. You take care of our horses. Eagle Feather and I will enter the tipi together and Flower Woman will welcome us." The young boy did as he was told. He didn't run the horses at a trot like he usually did. Instead he walked at a slow pace, head down, watching his moccasins taking a step ahead of him, as if he was not in the leather coverings.

Something has happened today. Perhaps Flower Woman can tell me?

When Bear Chief and Eagle feather walked through the temporary camp they were amazed at the number of Blackfoot tipis.

"There it is. My war bonnet is out by the flap on that heavy pole. Let's sneak inside through that open flap in the back."

"You go first." Eagle Feather said. "She might not see me in the darkness."

"Hum. I will change your powerful name to Chicken Feather if you back down." The men looked at the tipi, then at each other. "Cackle, cackle…"Or how about cock-a-doodle doo?"

"Who's out there? Show yourself. Is that you Little Bear? Come inside, *now.*"

"Wait, Flower Woman. Have you forgotten me already after only three days away from the village? Were you waiting for a Cheyenne brave to scratch your flap?"

The flap flew open and Flower Woman was in his arms.

"Bear Chief. At last you are here. I was wondering if you got lost somewhere." Then she saw Eagle Feather. She quickly dropped her feet to the earth. "Come in. Food is ready."

After eating a stew, Flower Woman had waited long enough to speak.

"We have had a wonderful time here. The blackrobes are friendly, welcoming people from all over the country. There are many different tribes here. White women are fussy about everything they do." She looked at Eagle Feather. "You will find them staring at you and giggling."

"Wait until they see me in the parade tomorrow morning. I have a true traditional costume to wear."

"What are you saying? Did you go shopping in Browning? You *will,* of course, wear your braids and your eagle feathers. That is your sign."

"So you say; so you say." I'll have to find another place to change clothes; paint my pony and braid his hair. Maybe Little Bear or Wise Owl will help me. I wonder where those two are.

The long ride finally caught up to Bear Chief. "Please fix me herbal tea. My back is sore." What I want is a steam, a pipe and quiet surrounding me. I suppose the drummers will continue for a while longer. By then, I'll be asleep in the robes with Flower Woman.

⸺◆◆◆◆◆⸺

33

T HE PRIESTS WERE up before dawn, had breakfast and were on their second cup of coffee. There was commotion in the yard every day and night since the anniversary celebration had begun. Today would try their very souls; hundreds wanted to be baptized. The Bishop, not realizing how cold the river water was, even in this hot summer time leading into an early fall, insisted on dunking those ready to receive this first Sacrament.

The main topic for the Bishop's sermon the day before had been about Baptism, and that all who received the Holy Sacrament would become Christians; Christ followers. The Father, Son and Holy Spirit came to hundreds; Indians and whites alike, filling the hearts of more than he had expected.

"This is a day to remember; are you two ready?" The Bishop walked over and looked out the window. "My coach awaits. The boys from the boarding school washed and polished it. Martha told me last night we are to lead the parade."

Father Jerome and Father Michael picked up the necessary kits used for such events and followed the Bishop out the door.

He was stunned to see Bear Chief standing in the yard, holding on to his horse's reins; dressed in his finest leathers. He wore the flowing war bonnet, used only for ceremonial purposes, and the chest plate, decorated with elk teeth.

Flower Woman sat proudly on her pinto next to him. She made a sign to Bear Chief. He raised his hand, palm up.

"Do you speak English?" asked the astonished Bishop.

"Do you speak Blackfoot?" Flower Woman knew he didn't.

The priests stared as Eagle Feather emerged from behind a large bush to sit his horse next to Flower Woman. He wore only an eagle feather in his braided hair and a loin cloth; beaded moccasins covered his feet. He was bareback on a horse with no reins or halter; main and tail covered in ribbons of all colors. Splashes of war paint decorated the shoulders of this powerful animal. Each splash recorded a victory coup for Eagle Feather. Flower Woman gasped and covered her mouth with her hand.

"Bear Chief, are you going to allow this man to dress this way?" asked Father Michael.

In the Blackfoot tongue Bear Creek spoke. "I have no control about what he wears. Let these newcomers to our land see the real Blackfoot Native. Not some reservation shut-in."

Eagle Feather did not interpret those words. Instead he said, "Eagle Feather is a warrior who fought many battles against the Blue coats. He is only dressed as a warrior today to repeat history for the newcomers who now work our land." He smiled and gave a sign of peace.

While this conversation was taking place on the far side of the yard, Martha and her family drove through the gate.

"Shriek! What is this? Who are you people?" She grabbed hold of her husband's arm and pulled him toward the priests. "Can you explain this?"

Father Jerome shrugged. "Martha. Good morning and welcome. We are gathering now for the parade. I see your buggy is decorated with large paper flowers and streamers. How festival it looks. Your dress is perfect for the occasion; wouldn't you say so, Bishop?"

Before he could answer, drummers began to chant to tribal members who wanted to be in the parade. Horses whinnied, the yard filled with Indians from several tribes.

Right on Army time a finely dressed group of soldiers, led by the Fort Commander wearing his ceremonial uniform and plumed hat, marched from the fort to the Mission's gate. When they heard the drummers they marched in place to the rhythm.

Even Martha, now settled down from her shock at seeing a Native Blackfoot atop a powerful horse was amazed at the colorful sight of the participants. "This day is for the history book; one we will all remember." *Surely there is a photographer in this crowd? Why did I not think of that?*

The roadside was jammed tight with horses, wagons and excited children. Guards from the fort had stationed themselves at every road crossing clear to the river. A volley of gunfire from the soldiers carrying rifles startled the horses. The parade was moving slowly down the road.

"Where are Little Bear and Wise Owl?" Bear Chief turned to Looking Back. She shook her head telling him she didn't know where the young men were hiding. Obviously they did not want to strut their horses in the parade.

The Army band played their company's song, *The Garryowen*. Many Irish soldiers followed the territorial governor, Thomas Francis Meagher, out west to help fight Indians. He proved to be a great war hero. In his memory, soldiers stuck sprigs of green from a near-by service berry bush into the bands of their hats. At the signal they moved as one on the road to the river.

Next in line was Martha's buggy. Her children clapped and waved as they passed by the crowds. Their mother had made hard candy and wrapped each piece in brown paper to keep it clean. Her children flung each piece out to the wagons watching their friends scramble for a piece of candy to suck on.

Due to some confusion, the Bishop's coach was stuck in the traffic and the driver cautiously placed his coach behind Martha's wagon. The brightly colored crumpled up paper looked like huge sunflowers on both sides of her wagon.

The Bishop rode in the coach, sitting on plush lined seats, curtained windows open. He waved and blessed the gathered.

Then came some ranchers who wanted to show off a horse or cow. The animals were penned into wagons for safety.

The crowd turned their attention to the next in line. Bear Chief, Flower Woman, Looking Back, their children rode abreast. Eagle Feather singled himself, thoroughly enjoying the chaos he created. Women turned their heads into husband's shirts, young girls waved and giggled only to be admonished by their mothers to stop. He gave signs, as his horse caught the fever and strutted; front hooves dancing.

We have the most beautiful horses on earth and mine leads the pack. Careful there old boy, don't you toss me into that crowd. The horse nickered and continued prancing down the road.

Lastly came the various tribes; Blackfoot women dressed in their best leather, beaded work on the sleeves and chest. Fringe cut precisely from the deer hide they had prepared for this occasion. With pride Bear Chief looked at his people. The white man is powerful. Could it be the Great White Spirit that gives them this power? We live under their rule in a reservation. My elders who remember these days are dying; the young born now think this is a day of fun. Who is right? Why can't we live in peace as we see fit?

Bear Chief shifted in his well-worn saddle and felt the stabbing pain in his back. *I must sit tall; show the white man he has not defeated us. He never will.*

The sun shone warm with a slight breeze; people brought up the rear with their wagons full of chattering voices. Soon they would all be gathered by the river. Baptisms would take several hours. The priests, already at the river crossing, stood ready to do their priestly duties. A choir from the parish church in the town of Ft. Shaw filled the air with beautiful songs befitting the day.

Father Jerome noticed the young Indian boys who were dangling their feet in the river, fishing for supper. I'm going to keep my eye on those two; there must be a reason for their behavior. No one else is fishing. The service is about to begin; later I'll have a talk.

Much to everyone's surprise the Bishop took off his black robe and waded into the water.

"Brr. You were right, Father Jerome. This river water runs cold." He laughed as he looked back to the shore line. He scooped up water and tossed it at a farmer who wanted to be baptized first on this special day. A big *Hooray!* Went up as the farmer took off his boots and cautiously stepped into the water.

"Brr!" he shouted back. The Bishop hurried him along and Father Jerome held the man at his back and shoulders. With a swift push his head went under and he came up sputtering.

"I baptize you in the name of the Father, Son and Holy Spirit"…

Martha jotted down names of those being baptized. She was so busy taking it all in that she failed to see Mary Fields standing in the shade under the bridge. Men who had received the Sacrament of Baptism took turns pulling people out of the water. The afternoon sun continued to shine and yet the line did not seem to grow smaller.

Father Jerome assisted the Bishop whose energy and stamina amazed him. He looked about for Father Michael and found him bent over near the river's bank. Mary stood at his side ready to help him.

"Father Michael, you need a break. I know you love doing God's holy work, but I want you to sit under the bridge with Mary in the shade and drink water. You will be needed again as this day turns into dusk."

"Harrumph! You think I can't stand up to the rigors of today? I love to see these souls cross into the arms of Jesus. Think how tired He must be receiving each and every soul we are sending to heaven at this very minute." He glared at Father Jerome but did go over by Mary to sit in the shade.

"Hello Mary. I didn't see you in the parade showing off the post office wagon."

"Didn' want to." She kicked a small stone into the river and watched it turn from a dull dusty colored rock into a gem stone. "Too bad those stones can't look that way all the time."

⬦─⬦─⬦─⬦─⬦─⬦

3 4

*F*ATHER JEROME SAT *on the river's edge delighted to see the line had finally ended. I don't remember ever being this tired or this wet. Why I didn't think to bring a change of habit, will remain a mystery. Even my sandals' feel squishy; but will have to do until I make it back to the Mission. His legs tingled from the brutal day of standing in the cold river water. The long walk home will at least put circulation back into this worn-out body.*

An older man with a wagon stopped to give him a ride but he refused. "Thanks, Joseph." He waved him on. "I need the walk. My legs have to limber up." The man slapped the reins over the horse's back and waved goodbye.

I sure hope God is watching and counting up this pain as a suffering for my eternal soul. Even Father Michael accepted a ride home with Mary in her wagon. By now he is probably dry and warm, sipping a cup of mint tea with a fancy cookie left over from last night.

Dusk was falling; tired families loaded into their wagons and headed for home. No community picnic was planned for the evening supper. Tonight the Bishop is to be the guest of Martha and what a meal that will be. She is an early homesteader to this valley and tends a huge garden. She will have sumptuous desserts at the ready for a treat later in the evening. I'm glad I was not invited. I just want to go back to the barn and sleep. There is work to be done at the Mission, too. Maybe the young men left early and as a surprise to me all the chores will be done, the cow milked, cream separator washed and the animals fed.

His tired legs carried him to the roadway where the Bishop's coach stood waiting. The Bishop, looking very tired but content, sat in the front with his coachman. The man had brought dry comfortable clothes for the Bishop to wear while visiting Martha's home.

The ride back to the Mission seemed such a luxury to Father Jerome that he almost crawled into the back seat of the coach. "You offer me a great temptation, your excellency. However, I am going to walk the rest of the way. Enjoy your evening."

Martha was already at the gate eager to greet her guest for the evening. The driver helped the Bishop transfer from the coach to Martha's still decorated buggy.

"Don't wait up." She laughed.

"That's not possible. I'll be asleep in the barn before you cross the lane to your homestead."

Martha gave a backhanded wave, clicked the reins and they were off.

When the buggy pulled into the yard, a barking, huge dog stopped at the buggy door keeping the Bishop at bay. He had not expected this. Martha yelled at the dog; her children came running to the front of the house; a cow wandered through the yard. A flock of ducks flew in unison up into the air, quaking and flapping their wings, flying right over the top of the buggy. The Bishop ducked, startled by the confusion. He turned to Martha. "Are all your welcomes this exciting?"

Tom, Martha's oldest child, grabbed the dog and opened the door for the Bishop. *What's next?* "Hello Tom. Thank you for assisting me."

"I'm to show you around the place. The two walked side by side down a stone path to a fenced in garden. We eat year round from this patch. Mom stores food in a dug out does a lot of canning in the fall. She don't waste nothin'."

The Bishop looked past the garden fence at the wheat fields turning golden heads to the sun. *How out of place all that green looks. Martha's Garden of Eden.* "I don't see any weeds."

"Mom has all us kids spend time in here early in the mornings.

Over here is our barn of sorts." He pointed to a three-sided lean-to with shovels, rakes, farm equipment, and muddy clothes hanging on hooks. "Pa plans to build a real one as soon as we get some money for our hay crops. That is going to put us over the top…if it don't hail."

"That wire fence place is where we keep the chickens in during the night. If we didn't, the foxes and wild animals would have them for breakfast." He laughed. "See that sign hanging on the fence gate? Mom made it. It says 'Stay smarter than the chickens if you want to eat a good Sunday dinner'."

"It takes time and strength and energy to live out here, I can see." Much different than city folks. I've learned a lot about my flock by coming here. I should not have waited all these years to share this adventure with so many. Yesterday was proof about how hungry they are for the Word of God.

Tom eventually returned to the house. Martha and two of her daughters were in the kitchen.

The Bishop noticed the bright yellow paint on the walls and a few herb plants sitting on the window sill. "I could smell something wonderful coming from this kitchen. Another minute away and I'd have been fighting Tom to get back to the house first."

When they sat at the kitchen table the Bishop noticed the fine silverware and fancy dishes. "Martha, where are you from originally?"

"Virginia. My father was a doctor. He had a wonderful practice. During the Civil War a dazed soldier came to the clinic and shot him. My mother found him behind his office desk; the berserk man standing over him with a pistol. He had gone a.w.o.l from the Union Army camped in a field not too far from our house. All he wanted was a glass of water and some food to put in his sack."

"How terrible for you to lose your loved one." He waited for more words from Martha.

"When the war ended my husband, who had been overseeing my father's slaves, decided to come out west. It was a good move. Montana Territory has changed since our first days here. We chose this area because of Fort Shaw. The renegade Indians burned us out more than once, but we were protected by the soldiers, and with their help things kept moving forward." Martha paused but only for a second. "We've been hailed out and had to worry about drought in the same season.

The winters are long, cold and harsh." She reached for her husband's hand. "My husband works very hard being a good steward of the land. He is known for his skills with horses and cattle."

Father Jerome was right. This woman can't stop talking. I am so tired and full from her delicious, meal; it has to end soon or I'll be yawning in her face, or fall face first onto the table.

"Martha, this was a lovely evening in your gracious homestead. Do you have your children enrolled at the Mission?"

"Oh, my yes." She turned her head and smiled with pride at her son. Tom serves Mass and helps teach Sunday School to the little ones. We try to make it every Sunday for church services, but sometimes the weather keeps us home. Trudging in four feet of snow with the wind always blowing can keep a body home by a nice fire." She looked at the children and her husband. He was not a talkative man but he smiled and drank a lot of coffee.

"We are learning from the good priests. They are very knowledgeable men. In return, I do help out as much as possible with inviting ladies to Bible study classes; do some chores, things like that." She picked up the empty bowls and platters and carried them to the dry sink.

"When those two first came here there was nothing. They have been very successful in building up the Mission. All tribes send sons to them. Now, they want to build a boarding house for young women. Sister Amadeus works with them during the days they are able to come. Some have great distances to travel." She put her hands on her hips.

"Are you here out of curiosity? Can you help us financially to build the school? Please don't say you are here to move the priests to a new location and let this mission flounder."

The Bishop was amazed at Martha's bold manner. He said nothing; yawned and stood up.

"Martha, it is time for me to return to the Mission. I plan to rest tomorrow and leave very early on Tuesday."

"Tom has the buggy ready. He will drive you back down the road." She smiled and did a little curtsy. "May I ask for a house blessing before you leave?"

"Why of course. I should have thought of that when I entered." With folded hands and closed eyes, he prayed for protection; health; love and peace to continue to fill the rooms.

ONDAY MORNING ALREADY? Can't they do something about that rooster? Then the Bishop heard more animal noises. He walked to the window; tossed back the heavy burlap shade and couldn't believe his eyes. A cat had curled up still sound asleep on his side of the wall; only to find a huge beast staring through the glass. What on earth? That must be the milk cow?

It is time for me to have a long, uninterrupted conversation I'd planned to do several days ago. No more celebration. I've got paper work to get finished and signed by these two very ambitious priests. They belong in another location; start another mission. California and the Jesuits are building the missions one after the other with great attendance. There work is spreading every seven miles.

Someone in the kitchen banged the bottom of a pan. "Come and get it or else it goes out to the chickens. A female voice laughed. "Father, we are ready with a good hearty breakfast after you hardly ate anything at Martha's house last night." More laughter, only this time it was cut short. Father Jerome and Father Michael frowned at the cooks.

He lightly dressed and put on his shoes, although he'd have preferred to wrap a lounging coat about himself and enjoy that first cup of coffee.

"That coffee does smell good. I'll be right there."

Several times they were interrupted during the meal. Young boys who worked at the mission came through the kitchen door, needing their work duties list, or asking about farm chores. Father Jerome stayed very positive through the interruptions and everyone seemed headed in the right direction for their daily activities.

The table, now cleared, became a writing desk for the men as they spread out paper and pencils.

"Your Excellency, why don't you begin with your questions?"

Father Jerome sat in his usual kitchen chair.

"Thank you. First of all, I want to tell you how much I enjoyed doing God's work these past days. Country living certainly has its own challenges, but the area is definitely populating this part of the territory. Statehood is sure to come soon.

The conversation abruptly changed. "I do have a serious question for you." He pulled out a letter from his shoulder bag. I received several of these letters recently about the woman you call Stagecoach Mary, or some call her Black Mary Fields. What is her place here at the Mission?"

The two priests looked at each other. "Her place? Why she helps us and Sister Amadeus with the school boys; she works very hard at whatever chore she faces." Father Jerome squirmed in his chair.

"Father, who wrote you those letters speaking badly about Mary?"

"I cannot reveal my source, but I must have her removed from this Mission. Tell Sister Amadeus to fire her." He read from a piece of paper; *"She drinks whiskey and she swears, and she is a…*he could not finish the sentence…*which makes her a low, foul creature."*

"Fire her? She has been here for years. Yes, she is a bit rough in her ways, but she does so much good, Father. This will break Sister's heart to have to tell her this news." Father frowned. "Why, it was Mary who brought the good sister back to health when she suffered from her lung disease. It is Mary who, rain, sleet, hail, snow, gets us our mail. She has done that for at least 8 years." He threw up his hands. "Why, the woman is now in her sixty's. What will she do if we don't keep her with us?" Father Jerome left his chair and walked to the curtained window. He could see Mary's cabin roof.

"I understand your problem. But see that it is done. I will send three young women to fill in from the Ursuline Order."

Tension filled the room. Finally, the Bishop stuffed his papers back into his black bag.

"Will you please get word to my driver that I want to leave very soon today? My work here is done. The reason for this trip is clear. As long as I am this far away from Helena, I might just as well check in with the Great Falls priests. It is a very large Diocese I have to cover."

Father Jerome was stunned by this sudden change of plans. He knew, however, that it was for the best. Apparently, the Bishop did not want to spend any more time with them.

"I'll get word to your driver. In fact, I think he might be getting oats from the barn now."

Father Jerome excused himself and with a sigh of relief hurried from the kitchen by way of the back door. He found the driver who was talking to several of the boys, delaying them from their chores.

"Hello, sir. I have a new message for you. The Bishop plans to leave very soon this morning and have you drive to Great Falls." He smiled at the surprised look on the driver's face.

"Tell him I'll be ready in less than one hour."

His driver waited patiently with the horse and coach. It was going to be a long, quiet ride eventually back to Helena; especially taking the route to Great Falls.

The parting was cool; hands were shaken; blessings came forth and then it was over. The weeks of planning: Ordering supplies, building stages, clearing a spot at the Sun River crossing for the Baptisms were now part of history and memory.

"Harrumph! I'm taking a nap; not to be disturbed. It will be a long while before we see another celebration around here like this one." Without another glance around the room, Father Michael headed for his own soft bed, not caring if the sheets were changed or not. *No more hay stacks for me.*

The horse clipity-clopped down the main partially graveled road past the Fort. Men at the gate saluted and stood at attention. Within minutes the ever-swirling dust cast its magic spell and the coach disappeared from sight.

When Father Jerome returned to the kitchen he looked into the meadow. Not a tipi pole still stood its ground. Without any fan-fair the tribes had moved out, going back to their way of life. *Dear God, what is to come of this? All I need would be Martha Sunshine wanting to talk.*

Two weeks passed before another letter came from the Diocese of

Helena. Mary delivered it in her usual fashion. Father Jerome put off opening it. *There is a weight to this letter that is pulling me down.* Finally at the insistence of Father Michael they opened the letter. One man read; the other listened.

"Two years, tops? Then we will be dismissed from this wonderful Mission we call home?" He couldn't believe it was going to happen. "Not a word of this do we discuss in public. Much can happen in that time frame and we must trust our Lord to direct our path." Father Jerome tried to remain optimistic. "Surely he won't abandon this place; these people.

The town of Fort Shaw is growing, maybe they want a permanent church built there. After all, we are receiving some financial help from the government. We cannot out-guess the reason, Father. Time will reveal it all to us."

"Harrumph!" What else does the letter say?"

"He asks if Black Mary is gone. I'll write him that she is gone from the Mission, but I won't write that she is the owner of a little café near here; that Sister Amadeus helped her make the transaction with the bank. He ends by thanking us again for our hospitality and for explaining the intricacies of living in the country. That's it."

He slapped the letter down on the table so hard his hand hurt.

⸻⬥⬥⬥⸻

36

T HE DOG RAN ahead of the old man on his horse. He sat at the closed gate, waiting.

"So. You want your own bed too?" He laughed at the dog whose tail wouldn't stop beating the ground. "It sure didn't take me long to remember why I left my post at Fort Shaw. I guess I was a tough old bugger back then, according to some of those old goats."

The dog, now impatient to run in his own space, barked wildly.

"Hold your britches there, boy. I'm right behind you. This place looks mighty welcome to me too." He opened the gate to let the dog sniff about while he unpacked his horse and put him into his pole corral. "Here's a welcome treat for you, too." He poured oats into a large bucket and set it on the ground.

He slept a while, only to be jarred awake by the scraping sounds of the travois on the upper road. Hmm. Must be Blackfoot people making their long journey to the reservation. That country is so beautiful and inviting. He walked to the edge of his fence and waved at the passing parade. One rider stood out from the rest. Why, there's that young brave I said hello to a couple of days ago. I didn't figure him to be Blackfoot. Too bad he doesn't speak English. I'd have enjoyed visiting with him more.

Little Bear pretended not to notice the old man and his dog. Something stirred inside him; he wanted very much to veer off the trail and stay with this strange white man. Flower Woman, always watching her child, caught Little Bear's hesitation; a chill went through her whole body.

154

She had seen this older white man talking to Little Bear, but because she was busy with the festivities, she put it out of her mind. *Who is he? Why is there an interest from Little Bear?*

I must talk about this to Bear Chief tomorrow. Could this be part of Little Bear's unhappiness this past week? Is he seeing things from his spirit guide? We must talk to him together. I will wait for the right time. Maybe Wise Owl knows something?

Flower Woman had not spent any time with soldiers from the fort. She saw no need.

The tired band moved past Bent's Fort. No one had things to trade and only a few in the group spoke the white man's tongue. They stopped for short breaks at little creeks to give water to the dogs and horses; they ate quickly from their own parfleche. Getting home took top priority over anything else. Thankfully, the loads on the travois were lighter making it easier for the dogs and horses to pull the left-over food stuffs. The horses were in good form after spending several days on the meadow grass at the Mission.

Flower Woman walked next to Looking Back. "Did you see Wise Owl and Little Bear talking to that old white man who lives in that cave we passed earlier today?"

"Those two were gone off on their own. I didn't pay much attention to who they talked with. Neither son speaks much English so I doubt much was passed, even in sign."

"Something isn't right. I am bothered. Will you keep me in prayer to help me find out what this is about? I feel an ill wind is going to blow into our tipi very soon." She shuttered. "Have you noticed how Bear Chief is not his usual self?"

"In what way, little sister?"

"Ever since we made the vision quest he has been quiet, wanting alone time. He talks to Eagle Feather more than you or me."

"That is true. Yes. There are changes. Why do you worry?"

"I don't like change, or surprises, or runners bringing him bad news."

"Things will be the same once we are home again." Looking Back took a drink of water from the elk's bladder. I hope she is not right this time.

Bear Chief is so much older than us. Maybe he is planning to make changes in who should be the next chief.

She turned to Flower Woman. "Please don't dwell on your evil thoughts. We are all healthy and busy. The children are growing up traditional, at least as traditional as we can remember it. Trouble comes to us from the evil one. We are near the reservation now. Don't let him into out tipis when we reach home."

"You are right as always, my sister. Being in our old homeland has stirred up forgotten memories. Let's try to remember we had a kind of a rendezvous this past week." She thought of something and grinned.

"The three blackrobes from the church thanked me for a delicious meal. I told them it was dog meat; and they immediately walked away from me; retching." Looking Back started to giggle and she put her hand over her mouth.

"Wasn't it fun to watch those old mountain men throw axes into cottonwood tree stumps?"

"Yes, but Bear Chief beat them all with his spirit-guided arrows. When he split his first arrow down the middle of its shaft with his second arrow, the young boys went wild. I even saw some women pretend they were scared of him." Laughter erupted and others turned to see what was so funny.

The reservation looked inviting, even in its poverty. Villagers were standing outside their tipis to wave their loved ones home. Little Bear wondered; *who will greet me home?* Bear Chief had left the celebration a day earlier than the caravan. He waited for Flower Woman and Little Bear to come closer to the tipi. Something was different. Little Bear shut his eyes. The old man in the cave came into his view.

<hr>

37

Little Bear and Wise owl made a plan to meet the following morning in the patch of trees and brush near the fence line of the reservation.

"Thank you for coming, Wise Owl. I have a question for you."

"You owe me one brother. It is six o'clock in the morning and here we are sneaking around in the woods. What's your question."

"How did I get this scar on my left wrist and arm? I've always had it; never thought it should not be there. I noticed it on you the last time we wrestled. You have the same scar on your right wrist and arm; it matches mine. We have different mothers. My skin is not as dark as yours."

"Whoa, right there, Little Bear! Yes, I have the same mark. You need to talk to Flower Woman and Bear Chief. I can tell you this much. "We have been blood brothers since the time you were born." Wise Owl didn't know what to do or to say.

"Why are you questioning the mark now? Did something happen at the celebration? We were together most all the time and I don't remember anything unusual." He paused for only a second. "Did that old white man say something to you? Something you weren't able to figure out what he meant?"

"No; he followed me around a lot. I'd see him watching me, studying me. That was why I stuck close to you most of the time." Little Bear stood tall. "Does Eagle Feather know things?"

"Sure. Like what?"

"Like this scar? Why I now feel something is not as it should be with me?"

"My gosh, Little Bear; you are my brother. What more do you need to know?"

"I want to learn to speak the white man's tongue and read his scratches he makes on paper. I want to go back to study at the Mission with the blackrobes." He coughed.

"Eagle Feather knows those things, yet he does not teach us. He and Bear Chief are closer than brothers. I want to know why."

"Talk to Flower Woman and Bear Chief before you do anything else. Then come back to me. You know we Blackfoot are very good at keeping secrets; there might be one about you?" Only your parents can help you. Go today before this thing gets way out of control."

"I am leaving now. Must bring in wood today for Looking Back. We have many days of work to catch up. Maybe you need to get busy; think about other things. Let our new Holy Spirit that came to us in Baptism lead your path and you listen."

Wise Owl ran through the meadow; relieved to be fleeing his blood brother. What is going to happen to Little Bear? He is brave and strong; he follows the traditions of our tribe. Why is he having these grown up thoughts? Why would he care about a bigger world?

Unable to put this behind him, Little Bear sought out Flower Woman. She was picking berry bushes; enjoying the peacefulness of being home. Little bear approached her from the front so as not to startle her and spill the basket almost full of rose hips.

"Good morning, Mother."

"Why, Little Bear, what a nice surprise. You called me Mother. It has been many seasons since you stopped saying that." She smiled up at him. "I remember when you told me you were now a grown brave and you would call me Flower Woman from that day on." She ran her hands down the apron covering her dress. "I couldn't decide if I should feel hurt or proud of your decision."

"I have a question that I can find no answers." His face frowned with confusion.

"Come sit and we'll talk." She patted the ground next to her.

"Where do I begin? Ever since the festive party at the Mission I have felt a stirring in my gut. The world opened up to me when I saw all the white people speaking to each other and I could not understand them. Some of the boys tried to make friends and even a few used hand signals they thought I would know."

Flower Woman remained very still and quiet. She did not reach out to touch the boy and she waited for him to continue.

"Then when I went inside the Mission House and saw the shelves filled with bound up paper, I asked the blackrobe about them. He told me they were called 'books'. He let me look at one and it had pictures of different Indian tribes from a place called 'back east' he called it. I used sign with the blackrobe."

Flower Woman nodded her head. He was talking about things she couldn't explain as her world was right here.

"We will ask Bear Chief and Eagle Feather to come to a special meal tonight. We will talk about this." She touched her hair. "Is this what bothers you?"

"There is more. I want to go to St. Peter's Mission and board there and learn the white man's tongue. I feel it is my next loop in my life." It all came out in a gush.

Flower Woman sat back on her hands; Little Bear thought she might faint. *Now look what you've done; you and your dreams of being somebody more than who you are. I must help her to the tipi.* "Here, let me take your basket and I'll walk home with you."

"Go find Eagle Feather and invite him to eat with us. I'm fine, just surprised by your new yearnings. Run along; I have work to do." Why did I insist on going to the celebration? We are all topsy-turvy and for what? For me to feel free; to see my baby's grave once again? Wise Owl must know what is bothering Little Bear. Well, first of all I must talk with Bear Chief. This will be a blow to him. I wonder if he ever dreamed such dreams?

Little Bear found Eagle Feather working as usual at his bench outside the tipi. He sat hunched over a piece of wood. His expectations of carving a long Eagle Feather with fine feathers kept him occupied; he was annoyed by the noise which meant interruption from his creative thoughts. Then he saw Little Bear. *That young brave grows taller and stronger every day.*

"Flower Woman invites you to Bear Chief's tipi for supper. Come anytime but we eat by dusk." He spurted out the sentence, whirled around on his toes and ran back down the path.

I wonder what's under his craw. I guess I am going to have one of Flower Woman's special meals tonight. That always means something important is about to take place.

•———•◆•◆•◆•◆•———•

38

T HE OLD UNION soldier, who retired as Commander from Fort Shaw ions ago, was disturbed. He had spent time at the fort; met other soldiers from his era and attended only a few of the festivities jam-packed into a long weekend. At the parade route passing in front of the St. Peter's Mission, he stood dressed in his parade uniform, happy to have the wide brimmed hat with the plume. It was nearly noon and the sun was high, the reunion buddies were trying to look sharp in their tattered, ill-fitting uniforms. They saluted flags in the parade; slapped each other on their backs. His heart wasn't in it. He decided to go to his cave earlier than scheduled by the committee.

After a good sleep in his own surroundings, he drug out the trunk once more to hide the past from his sight. *Probably be only one more time I wear that outfit again.* He felt a pang of sadness pass through him.

I could pack up and go back east. Why don't I? Why? Because there is nothing back there for me. My family is all crossed over by now. I never hear from any of the nephews; my brother's gone. Best I just stay right here. I don't want to be a burden to strangers.

We all, soldiers and Indians alike, have too many memories of a very rough time to be out here on these high plains. Children born today will only think of those days gone by as a time to have a party. Only a few of us reprobates still around; many living in the caves like I do. I see civilization creeping like an eight-legged monster grabbing, sweeping the land for more settlers. He shook his head, his hands, and kick-stepped each leg. This rheumatiz is doing the same thing to me.

His thoughts stayed on the anniversary activities. That young Indian brave that I tried to talk to sure isn't all Indian. His father is Bear Chief; he told me his name was Little Bear. He couldn't understand English, yet he seemed eager to learn. Next time I'm at Bent's Fort I'm going to ask around. Might be something there. Naw. He's probably got some white in him, but that's no concern of mine. He's a reservation injun.

He looked back at the stump table. He'd overlooked returning the calico material he had worn around his neck for some of the events. He picked it up and kissed it. *I guess I'll leave this out; put it on that little table where the Bible is.*

❖

LITTLE BEAR WATCHED Flower Woman prepare the special dinner. He had no appetite and he couldn't keep his legs from twitching. *Where is Eagle Feather? Why does he have to be here? No need for him to interpret what we say. Yet Flower woman sent me to find him.* He frowned as many thoughts raced through his mind.

At last he is scratching on the flap. Little Bear jumped up to open the flap.

When he saw Eagle Feather he was stunned. Before him stood a proud warrior, dressed as if going into battle. He had papers in his vest pocket. Little Bear saw arrows with red and black feathers on the pointed sticks in the long woven basket strapped to his back.

Before he could say anything, Flower Woman signed welcome to Eagle Feather. He signed back. Then Bear Chief signed welcome to him. Not a word filled the tipi walls. Little Bear stood alongside Eagle Feather totally confused.

Flower Woman led their guest to his place across from Bear Chief. Suddenly the adults started to laugh. "Wasn't that fun, Little Bear? Did you understand our signs?"

"Yes, I understood the signs. I did not understand why you greeted each other in that way." He pointed to Eagle Feather. "Why is he dressed for war? Is this your way of telling me there is a war coming to our people? Little Bear brought his eyes to a slit and looked at Eagle Feather. "I see great bravery and pride in your life. Are you content being a Blackfoot?"

Eagle feather remained silent. This was something that needed to be answered by Flower Woman. A decision after their conversation would come from Bear Chief. The baby they all loved was no longer an infant; a word from Bear Chief would seal his fate. *He will learn, like I did, and be in line as our next Chief.* Many secrets were about to be spilled into the center circle.

"I spoke to Bear Chief after you left me. We want to hear it from you in Blackfoot tongue what it is you want to add to your life. What happened at the Mission?"

Little Bear squirmed and sat cross-legged on the woven mat. "I don't know where to begin. I have feelings that won't go away inside my head. This is not new. I feel like my life began way before the reservation move you speak about. Sometimes I think I belong somewhere else." He coughed.

"I know of no other place than this village. Then I saw the books the blackrobe showed me at the Mission. I am grown now, almost a man. I want to leave here, only for a while, and study with the blackrobes. They can teach me English and how to write on paper. I want to read those books on their shelves. There is a boarding school for Indian boys and I can help with chores."

Bear Chief stared at his war bonnet; walked to it and put it on his head.

"Are you proud of me when you see me wear this bonnet?"

"Yes. You are a great chief of many years. You have knowledge about other things. You are my father and nothing will change that."

Bear Chief took off the bonnet and returned it to its stand by the flap.

He left the tipi and walked to the edge of the river. His thoughts drifted with the twigs floating in the water. Why does the river always flow away? Why does Little Bear seek the ways of white man's world? I ask you Great Spirit to send answers. If I let him go will he fly to his white man's nest? Or will he return satisfied with what he learned? If he becomes the next Chief, knowing white man ways would be necessary for talk of peace and treaties; benefits for the Village. Bear Chief began to wail. His sound floated on the current away from all he knew.

Flower Woman came to his side. She did not touch him or speak. He felt her presence and that brought comfort.

"Eagle Feather, why are they gone so long?"

"They are praying to the Great Spirit and to the Holy Spirit. They will return with answers. I will stay here with you." Eagle Feather dug out the papers from his vest pocket. He unfolded them and started to read in English, then returned to Blackfoot.

I cannot understand it. Eagle Feather brought those papers to support me; that I need to learn this strange way of talking and writing. Why? What is this about, Eagle Feather?

"Many seasons ago when I was about your age, I sought for truth, like you are doing now. I spent a winter with a mountain man. He taught me how to trap fish, shoot a fire stick, be independent and listen to my heart. The head mixes us up. The heart holds the key to what bothers us. After that winter when snow turned to rain, I came back to my people. I listened to my heart and made the right choice for me. Now you have to make that choice for you."

They sat in silence, waiting, waiting, waiting for that flap to open. Little Bear, now calm, would accept, for now, whatever his father would tell him. But he knew he would listen to his heart, one day riding away from all he knew and loved.

At last the flap flew open. Bear Chief came in first, trying to hold back tears.

"We have talked to the Great Spirit. Little Bear you may attend the Mission School starting this journey into the white man's world. Flower Woman and I have talked tonight. We prayed for answers. "You may pick one of my best horses and find your way back to the Mission." He sighed deeply. "I will send Eagle Feather now to bring back papers. When he returns and we know you are safe with the blackrobes, then you must leave."

Eagle Feather was surprised at this answer. When I wanted to go off and explore, Bear Chief opposed the idea. Maybe he has regretted his decision about me. I found answers, but I came back to the tribe. I wonder if Little Bear will make the transition from Indian to white boy? He will live with Indian boys at the school, for sure, but he still will have to fight his way. I only hope he knows how to do that.

"Tonight Eagle Feather came dressed as a warrior. He has a story to tell you about his life choices." Bear Chief sat down cross-legged on his mat. "He has an Indian heart and one day will rise to be our Chief."

Little Bear had never thought about who would lead this village. It startled him to think Bear Chief was getting old. No one pays attention to such things until a crisis unveils the reality. Flower Woman would need help.

"He already told me about living away from the tribe with the mountain man. Wise Owl will always be near to help Flower Woman and Looking Back; he does so now." Little Bear looked at Flower Woman. "I am only asking for time away for a few seasons. I am curious about the power of the Whiteman's government."

Eagle Feather waited his turn to speak. Doing so, he pulled out the packet of papers he had stored in his pocket. "Remember the two white-men who came to visit and Flower Woman ran them off?" He paused. "They were from the government, yes. They left these papers with me. They are forms and information about an Indian School that takes Indians off the reservation to teach them the way of civilized peoples. It is called the Carlisle Indian Industrial School and it is far away in a state called Pennsylvania. They wanted to find young men and take them from here to board with them." Eagle Feather shoved the papers toward Bear Chief. "Little Bear can go to the Mission School and learn white man ways there. Then if he should want to learn more he can apply for entrance at this school. If you do not want these papers then toss them into the fire."

Little Bear picked up the packet. "I'll keep these safe in my medicine bundle. We can see if the power grows stronger in a closed bag." He ran to the hook, brought it back to the group and opened the strings. He noticed a strip of calico material mixed in with the berries and other items Flower Woman added each year. He was too excited to give the cloth any attention. He folded the packet to fit the bag; closed the draw strings and returned the medicine bag with the beaded bear design back to the sacred hook. He had never opened the bundle; always it was Flower Woman who added treasures to his guides and powers.

"I'll leave tonight and bring you back the message from the blackrobes." With that said Eagle Feather slipped out the flap and disappeared into the now dark night.

"Bear Chief, Little Flower, thank you for listening to my request. If I do leave you it will only be for a little while; you will forever be in my heart."

"We have kept a secret about Eagle Feather for many reasons. I am going to tell you now. Eagle Feather is my blood brother. When our father died, Eagle Feather was gone into the mountains. The elders appointed me to follow in my father's way." Flower Woman put her hand on Bear Chief's arm.

"It was a struggle between us for some time. I made a vow with the help of my Great Spirit's guidance that if something comes of me Eagle Feather will succeed as the next Chief of the Blackfoot Nation here on the reservation."

"You do not know of such things at your young age." He paused and looked at Little Bear. I do not want to see you and Wise Owl quarrelling over you leaving and him staying."

"But Wise Owl doesn't want to leave his home. He wants to be here with family. He trains young boys to ride, to hunt and fish. He pretends he will be a sub-chief one day."

"How do you know this?"

"We talk. Wise Owl has taught me everything since I was born about such things."

"And you? What do you dream about?"

"I have mixed dreams. Sometimes I am a leader of white men; I live far away. These dreams frighten me because I do not fit in with that world."

"Listen to your Chief." Your mother and I give you our blessing. You must follow your heart." He crossed his arms and hit his chest with his fist.

"That is what Eagle Feather told me tonight. But how can I follow my heart if I don't know the path. That is why I have to go to the mission. I have to find that path."

41

Eagle Feather had changed his clothes. He wore jeans and a cowboy shirt with fancy button. The secret trails cut off many miles as he passed by Bent's Fort, continuing at a fast gallop towards the Old Man Who Lived In A Cave. He would stop there for water for him and his horse.

The old man, fishing for supper, heard his dog growl.

"Looks like we've got company, old boy. Behave yourself now."

The dog barked, neither welcoming nor happy to see the intruder.

Eagle Feather recognized the animal from the past few days at the Mission. The dog had wolf in him, no doubt. He stopped at the gate, raised his hand to the old man and waited for a reply.

"Come on in; set yourself on a stump."

Eagle Feather slid off his horse; with reins in hand he approached the old man.

"I am Eagle Feather, from Bear Chief's village on the reservation. May I water my horse?"

"Welcome to whatever I have." He walked up from his fishing hole, dangling several nice trout. "Stay and rest a while. Your horse looks tired. I've got fish." He held up his string.

"You speak pretty good English for an injun."

Eagle Feather cringed. *Will there ever be a change in how white men think of us?* "Thank you, yes. I would like to eat your fish."

"Didn't I see you at the Mission last week?" The old man took a sharp knife and whacked off the fish head, then slit it open. He took out the innards; tossed them into the dog's dish.

"Yes, I was there. I saw you many times."

The fish fried in the bear grease and Eagle Feather realized he was hungry. It had been almost a full day since he had eaten. The old man set raw vegetables from his garden in the center of the table. The aroma of sour dough bread wafted out of his oven. Two cups of fresh coffee, special from Bent's Fort and saved by the old man for special occasions, tempted Eagle Feather to start eating before his host. Out of respect for the meal, he waited for the host to sit down. They ate fast and in silence. This was not a social call for either of them.

"Thank you, sir. The meal was very good. Now I must be on my way to the Mission before morning." Eagle Feather left the cave and found his horse. In one jump he swung easily onto the back of the animal. He gave an Indian sign for goodbye. Both man and dog watched the beautiful sight of the Indian as he leaned forward over the horse's mane, once again galloping toward his goal of reaching the Mission. *I wonder if that man is Little Bear's father. I saw the cloth on the table. It matches the strip Flower Woman put in Little Bear's bundle. Is now the time to tell Bear Chief of this? His faithful horse never broke stride as they continued down the now recognized trail.*

Good. There is light in the window of the Mission. He galloped through the gate and jumped to the ground. Dogs barking alerted the priests.

"Harrumph! Who can that be at this time of night? Even the roosters are still asleep."

Father Jerome went to the door, surprised to see Eagle Feather.

"Come in, come in. What brings you to our door?"

"I am Eagle Feather from Bear Chief's village. May I enter?"

Father Jerome swung the door open wide; Eagle Feather stepped inside the house.

He looked around, seeing comforts of nice chairs, shelves filled with books; a pot of hot tea on the table top, along with a pastry of some sort.

"Sit here. I'll get another cup and you can have some tea with take a scone. Martha from the ranch down the road made them."

Eagle Feather did not hesitate. He sat at the table and stared at the other priest. These two men alone have built this Mission from nothing almost twenty years ago. I remember the night they came to our camp in that screeching cart. They were very nervous to be among us. I wonder if they still are afraid of Indians now that they have learned some things about us.

"I come bringing a message from Bear Chief. His son, Little Bear, wants to come here. He is raised as a reservation Indian; knowing only about this Blackfoot way of life. He wants to learn white man tongue and read the scratches you make on paper. He is curious. He is a good boy." Eagle Feather carefully lifted the delicate china cup to his lips and swallowed the hot tea.

Father Jerome looked at Eagle Feather. "You speak English and I would suppose you can read and write words."

Eagle Feather laughed. "I learned English from a mountain man one winter. I am never sure of my words and what I am saying. Little Bear and Wise Owl both have heard me speak when I am angry. When they were younger they would run and hide behind my wood pile until I cooled down."

"What about Little Bear's parents? Do they know of his desire to come here?"

"Yes. Bear Chief sent me. They both agreed to let him come here if there is room."

Father Jerome tried not to show his delight at this news. "I watched Little Bear last week and tried conversing with him. I showed him a book. He could not put it down."

The priests looked at each other. There was no need to discuss. The future of this boy was in their hands.

"Without a doubt we will welcome Little Bear. When can we expect him?"

"I can say within seven moons. He is excited and wants to come."

"Then it is settled. Please wait while I find a form for you to give to him for his signature and possibly your signature, too." He left the chair and went to a cabinet where he found the papers. He folded them and put them into an envelope and handed the envelope to Eagle Feather.

"We will tell Sister Amadeus she has a new student. He will sleep on a cot in the barn with other boys. It is called a dormitory. There will be chores. He is free to return home to visit after the fall harvests are complete and before the snow covers us. He can keep his own horse in the meadow."

Eagle Feather crossed the parlor floor, opened the front door and mounted his horse. As quietly as he had come, he disappeared into the darkness of night.

It was nearly day break when the old man heard a horse galloping on the upper trail. His dog stood guard at the care entrance, but the sound of the horse's hooves passed on by. *I wonder what's the big hurry.*

Eagle Feather never seemed to tire while on a mission for his brother. I am happy now that Little Bear knows our secret. I wonder if Flower Woman will tell him the secret she has carried all his life. There must be a reason for the Great Spirit to put this desire into Little Bear's heart. I'll do what I can to help him understand his birth if he needs to talk about it.

Wise Owl certainly has kept his vow to never reveal that secret. He is well named. I wonder if Little Bear has ever asked him about their matching scars? Maybe he thinks it is a birthmark they both carry?

The trip went fast. Eagle Feather went straight to the tipi of Bear Chief. He smelled smoke and coffee.

Ah! The house is awake. I'll scratch the flap. Flower Woman will feed me. Maybe I'll tease Little Bear and not tell him anything until after we eat.

It was torture for Little Bear who sat patiently beside Eagle Feather. Why is he not speaking of his mission? Has he good news? Do they not want me? I have to know…now.

At last the meal ended. All eyes turned to Eagle Feather. In Blackfoot, loud enough for all circled in the tipi, he spoke.

"The blackrobes said yes to your requests. They will have a cot ready in a room called a dormitory. It is in the barn and there are other boys sleeping there. You will help with chores; study books."

Eagle Feather handed the form to Little Bear. "You have to sign your name. I will help you." He made an X; Little Bear did the same.

"Thank you my brother." Bear Chief reached for Flower Woman's hand. He spoke to her in native tongue. "We are agreed?" She shook her head. "He must take the trail from here by himself; find things we shielded him from including his birth; learn things we cannot teach him."

He stood up and pulled Flower woman to his side. They both took a hand and pulled up Little Bear to stand with them. "I am proud to call you my son."

"Go, Little Bear. You must find what it is you seek. Let the Great Spirit guide your path. Take my horse…as a gift from me. He will take you to the place you want to go. Flower Woman has packed a basket full of food for you eat on the trail." He grabbed the basket and handed it to Little Bear. "Never forget all you have learned from your mother. She is a very wise woman."

Suddenly, both parents and Eagle Feather turned their backs to Little Bear. He was being shunned. Startled by their action, he grabbed his few possessions and stuffed the papers, forgotten on the table, into his bag that held a few clothes, his winter coat, gloves, hat and a pair of moccasins. He did not look back or say a word. Confused, he stepped through the tipi flap.

Immediately he felt free. He found the horse behind the tipi, wearing Bear Chief's saddle.

He tied his bundle with leather straps. Positioning the clothes sack took some time as balance was important for the horse's gaits. He raised his left foot and slid it into the stirrup. The right leg automatically flew over the saddle. In one swift movement he gave a gentle kick to the horse's ribs.

Flower Woman heard the hooves. Only then did she go outside. One last glance at the backside of her baby; now a young brave; imprinted forever in her heart. Suddenly, she had a flash back to another night when the stars shone brightly overhead. Falling stars showered her and she instinctively knew something was going to change her life forever.

White Owl had decided when Little Bear told him he wanted to leave the reservation and attend the Mission School that he would trail him in secret to make sure he found his way. To Wise Owl, this was an attempt to see Little Bear take another first step into his world. He waited in a grove of trees until Little Bear disappeared from sight. He had not mentioned any of this to Looking Back. *She will understand when I come back in two moons.*

What in thunder is goin' on? Here comes another injun riding on the upper trail. I've left my flag out. Might bring me some more company. When the horse got close enough for the old man to see the rider he was surprised. It was that same kid he'd tried to talk to at the Mission. *Wonder why he is travelin' alone and toward the Mission. Sure hope Bear Chief is not injured or ill.* The rider did not stop and the old man went back inside his cave.

About an hour passed when he heard another horse on the upper trail. Too much traffic on that trail any more. All that comin' and goin' is makin' me grumpy and nervous. I don't like not bein' in the know about stuff that might concern me. Those injuns might be passin' war plans to other warriors to attack the homesteaders. The guards at the fort better be on the alert. I knew that party would bring nothing but trouble. He stayed outside a while longer until it was quite dark and he felt safe that there would not be any more disturbance. He reached down and patted the dog's head. "Good boy, you keep watch. I'm goin' inside. Gotta check my pistol."

At the top of the hill Little Bear stopped and dismounted. He guessed it was too late for him to go calling. He checked the sky and decided dawn would be breaking soon and he could stay where he was for a couple of hours.

He had no idea his friend, Wise Owl, watched him at a distance. This was a hard time for Wise Owl. He did not want to lose his best friend, his blood brother, yet he had no words that would stop him. *Little Bear has to find his own place. I found mine. We will always be together, only in a different way.*

Lights came on in the Mission kitchen. That was the sign Little Bear had waited to see.

He rode his horse down to the Mission gate and dismounted. He walked up the path, feeling as if he were taking his first baby steps like a toddler. He knocked three times on the door and Father Jerome opened it wearing a kimono-type robe and a big smile.

"Step inside. We've been waiting for you." Little Bear did not enter. "First I want to leave my bundle, then I must tend to my horse. I'll come back after I turn him loose in the meadow."

42

Classes started that same day for Little Bear. People were friendly; some giving him tips on how to survive the changes that were about to take place. He sat, rather timidly watching, listening to the white man tongue. It fascinated him to see writing that others in the room knew what the scratches said and what they meant. *Will I ever catch on to this? Am I the only one who doesn't know what it says or means? I'm trying not to wiggle or move my eyes. The blackrobe keeps looking my way. Why? Am I doing something wrong? I have to go to the bathroom. What do I do about that? I'm getting thirsty, too. Where is my horse?*

"Little Bear. Wake up and listen. You will never learn if you wander in your thoughts."

Little Bear heard a voice scolding him. It seemed very far away. He sat up straight.

Finally the teacher called for a break. All the children half ran to the outhouse and Little Bear followed since he didn't know what else to do.

"Little Bear; come here to me." Father Jerome motioned to him to stand in front of him.

"These first few days will seem a bit confusing and I know you don't understand me now, but you will; very soon. I am going to tutor you. In the future, you are to call me Father Jerome. No more blackrobe name, understand? Father Jerome tried to make signs that Little Bear could read. Some warm feelings spread through the bewildered young

Indian brave who wondered if he had done the right thing by coming here; by leaving what he knew.

Within a week Father Jerome had advanced Little Bear to speak, recognize and read a few words: hello, goodbye, thank you, please, yes and no. He had him repeat the list of words over and over until he had them memorized.

Little Bear studied hard every free minute he had. He talked to his horse every day; first in Blackfoot fearing that the horse would not understand English; then in English. He wanted more than anything to be one with his horse, the Blackfoot way.

Fall season had been good to the homesteaders. The fields yielded abundant crops and the hay came in two cuttings. Little Bear was homesick and Father Michael worried about him.

Many moons flew by. The weather started to give hints that winter snows and cold would soon swallow him. He decided it time to return to Bear Chief's tipi for a visit.

"Father, please sir. I want to go. I want to visit my parents. Much to discuss. I want to return to you."

"When?"

"Today. I need four moons." Little Bear spoke in English but mixed the signs and symbols of his native tongue.

"Leave when you are ready. We are going to dismiss everyone for one week; seven moons. It is called a school recess. Farm children are needed to help bring in the family hay, prepare animals for sale, bring in the gardens and wood."

"Thank you, sir. I will return soon."

It actually felt good to be on the back of his horse, riding the trail towards the old man's cave. I am going to stop there and ask for water for my horse. Maybe he will invite me to eat since I now can speak a little bit of English to him.

The faithful dog barked loud and long before Little Bear rode up to the gate.

"Who's there? What do you want?" Came a voice from inside the cave.

"It is Little Bear; son of Bear Chief. I want to speak."

Why that's the Injun kid. He's talking English. "Let's talk. Coffee's hot. Water your horse in the pole corral."

"Hello." Little Bear signed Peace. "Thank you for the coffee."

Little Bear looked around the inside of the cave and was amazed at how orderly and comfortable everything seemed to be. He saw books on a shelf among other things.

"I am learning white man ways at the St. Peter's Mission. I love to read."

"Take a walk around my humble home, kid. Glad you stopped by."

It was then that Little Bear saw the piece of calico material that was spread over the small table with the kerosene lamp and the Holy Bible decorating it. *Where have I seen that cloth? I must ask Flower Woman if she knows.*

"Sir, where did you get that calico cloth?"

A sadness furrowed across the old man's face. "Why do you ask?"

"It is pretty to look at."

"Anther time we'll talk about that cloth. Not today. Do you like to fish? I was getting' ready to sit on the bank." He motioned to Little Bear to follow him.

"Thank you sir. Another time I will fish with you. I must be on my path. I want to visit my family on the reservation before it snows." Little Bear stumbled on some of the words, but the old man understood him.

"Then be on your way."

"Yes, sir. I will return to you in five moons or less." He went to his horse and the two melded into one. Little Bear did not fear the white man, but he felt something…no word could describe it. He let out a war whoop and sped on down the trail.

The old man never made it to the fishing hole. He dropped his pole in the dirt and returned to the cave. He went to the piece of calico cloth and held it in his hands; then he started weeping. *There is something about the Injun kid. I'm goin' to find out what it is.*

At first sight of the reservation Little Bear urged his horse into a gallop. *I'm home.*

"Flower Woman," shouted Little Bear. "Where are you?"

Flower Woman stopped in her tracks. She was walking between the two tipis; visiting with Looking Back. She heard her name.

"Little Bear? Is that you or is the coyote playing tricks with my ears?"

"Here I am, Mother." He slid from his horse and ran to her. "I am home for a few days. I can speak English. Of course, Flower Woman did not understand the words, but she knew her son had come home. She would send one of her children to find Eagle Feather and tell him to come to the tipi.

"Come inside. I give you herbs to drink to strengthen you from your journey.

She shouted for Looking Back to send one of her children to Eagle Feather and tell him to come to her tipi.

"It is good, Mother. I find school good."

Eagle Feather came running, not knowing what to expect. He rushed through the flap when he saw Little Bear's horse standing at the entrance."

"Flower Woman, are you…" Eagle Feather stopped mid-sentence when he saw Little Bear.

"Ah, it is good. Hello my nephew. You are smiling. Everything is good with you?"

"Yes, Eagle Feather. I like school now that I can understand words in English."

He stood up and went for an embrace from Eagle Feather. Just then Bear Chief walked inside the tipi. "Little Bear, is that really you? I have been having dreams about you." He put his arms around his son. "All is well? Why are you here today? Speak our tongue."

"Hello, my father. I am fine. I can speak some English. Books are very difficult, but the blackrobes help me; I am learning very fast. I am happy there." The boy smiled. "I am on a good path and will return to the Mission in two moons from now."

"I must find Wise Owl. Where is he?"

"You will find him at the wood shed cutting wood for our winter that will be upon us soon."

Little Bear left the tipi and searched for his friend.

"Wise Owl. There you are, busy as usual."

Wise Owl dropped the ax and the two best friends slapped each other on the back.

"Did you find you are not smart enough to learn the white man's tongue and you are back home where you belong?"

"No such thing, Wise Owl. I am here to visit. I missed you. I have questions and I think you have answers. Can we talk?"

"Yes. Sit on that stump. No one is near to hear us. What do you want to talk about?"

"Yesterday I stopped at the old man's cave. He gave me coffee. I looked around his home. I saw a calico cloth on a table. Somewhere I know I have seen that same cloth, but I don't know where or when."

Wise owl did not move. Do I send him away with some excuse; tell him I know nothing about the calico cloth? I have a strip in my medicine bag and he has one in his bag. I promised Bear Chief in a vow I would never reveal the secret. Spirit Guide I need you beside me.

"We go together; get your medicine bag. Answers are there. Flower Woman can talk to you." Wise Owl started to walk away.

"Wait, Wise Owl. What will she talk to me about?"

"Follow me. I must stop for my medicine bag."

When the two young men entered the tipi, Flower Woman felt their anxiety. *Has the time come to reveal our secret about Little Bear?*

"Sit. Drink tea. Talk to me." She smiled. Then she noticed Wise Owl carried his sacred bag carefully in his hand.

"Flower Woman, the time has come for Little Bear. Talk to him."

She went to the sacred pole and took down both her medicine bag and Little Bear's bag.

"Open your bags and pull out what you are looking for." She put her bag next to her leg.

Wise Owl and Little Bear both reached into their bags; both pulled out the strip of calico cloth. Flower Woman then opened her bag. She also pulled out the piece of cloth.

"I saw this cloth at the old man who lives in a cave's room. What does this mean?

Why do we have strips of this cloth? I am confused? He frowned. "Flower Woman do you know this white man?"

Flower Woman shook her head. "No. I do not know him."

"Then, why...?"

"Shhh... I want to tell you a story." All three sat together in a tight circle. Flower Woman began to speak. Little Bear could not believe what his ears were hearing.

E AGLE FEATHER, ALREADY visiting the tipi of his brother, Bear Chief, decided to stay. His spirit guide, the eagle, flew very close to the tipi as if sending a sign he would be needed.

Flower Woman opened the calico cloth; showed Little Bear the ripped edges; took his strip and carefully fitted it into place. She did the same with Wise Owl's piece. The two braves watched silently as if seeing a puzzle for the first time.

"Wise Owl found you when you were only a few hours old. Your mother, for reasons we do not know was alone up in the high prairie on the trail to Fort Shaw. She was dead. Somehow, before she died, she ripped off her skirt and wrapped you into a bundle for protection." She had to take a deep breath in order to continue.

"Wise Owl brought you to Bear Chief. That same night I delivered a still-born boy. He is buried on our homeland not too far from the fort. Bear Chief put you into my arms. My bitter tears turned into shining eyes. We decided to keep you a secret because we did not know what would happen if we took you to the fort. I wanted you with all my heart." She reached out to touch Little Bear. He sat as solid as a Cottonwood tree stump.

Eagle Feather knew this story well. He had been Bear Chief's top warrior at that time; running special missions. He had no problem interpreting this unfolding story. *Little Bear is hearing another secret. Mine revealed a few months ago; now this very complicated one.*

"It was another time, Little Bear. The Bluecoats soldiers were patrolling every day. Rogue Indians were starting skirmishes everywhere. We could not prove where you came from. We did not want to bring a war upon the Blackfoot tribe of Bear Chief. We did not want to be blamed for the woman's death."

She turned to Eagle Feather. "Bear Chief sent Eagle Feather to find out what he could about the woman. She was the Commander of the fort's wife. We did not want any bad thing to happen to you, so we hid you." She turned to Wise Owl.

"Wise Owl, tell him about the scar on his arm that matches yours."

Wise Owl did not hesitate. "I wanted you for a brother. You were days old. I was around eight seasons old. I cut my vein and I cut your vein. I rubbed my blood into your vein. We are blood brothers. You have Indian blood in you. So many times I almost told you, but I made a vow to Bear Chief."

Little Bear was confused and having a very difficult time grasping this story.

"I am a white man's child? But I look and talk and feel Indian."

Flower Woman spoke again. "For that we are grateful to the Great Spirit. We have all cared for you. Looking Back is like a mother to you. She kept the secret all these years. In fact, we had forgotten about it. You wanting to learn white man's ways must be deep in your soul. That is why your father and I agreed to let you find your way."

Eagle Feather kept talking, making signs, wanting to get this settled. He remembered the pain he felt those many years ago.

"This is a shock to you. But that is the story we know. You have grown to be a mighty fine brave. We believe in the Indian tradition of one choosing a blood brother."

Little Bear needed to be alone to think.

"I leave now. The man in the cave also has this cloth. I must talk to him. Is it possible he is my father?" With that, Little Bear jumped up and walked through the flap. The three left inside were not surprised at his actions. "Let him go. He must find his way," said Eagle Feather.

The old man heard the horse before his dog started barking. Little Bear did not wait to be welcomed. He jumped to the ground; ran looking for the man and found him at the river's edge.

"Are you my father?" Little Bear shouted at the man.

"Kid, are you all right? Did those Injuns give you loco weed? What?"

"No. My mother gave me this." He thrust out his hand full of the calico cloth. "This."

"What in tarnation are you goin' on about?"

"Do you know who I am? Is that why you stalked me at the festival? Were you going to tell me a story?" Little Bear backed away from the man. In broken English he tried to make his words be clear.

"What is my white man name? Were you the commander of the fort?"

The words tumbled over each other as Little Bear continued to shout them out.

The big dog went to Little Bear and placed his head on Little Bear's hand just above the wrist; he whined and was trembling.

"Get away from me." He swung his arm toward the dog, but he did not try to hit him.

The break gave the old man the chance he needed. He grabbed Little Bear and clutched him to his chest.

"Calm down, kid. We need to talk. I don't know the Indian side of this story, but I can tell you my side. You need more of the pieces to understand what has happened to you.

Little Bear felt the genuine warmth and concern coming from a beating heart.

"Tell me. Who am I?"

"I don't know who you are. Let's try and figure this out." He put his arm around Little Bear's shoulder and led him inside the cave where it was comforting and warm. Little Bear sat on one of the crude chairs. The old man went to the table and lifted the calico cloth. He held it up next to the strip that Little Bear finally gave up to him.

"Yes, by golly. They do match. I've always believed you were alive. That is why I never went back east when my command was taken over by a younger soldier. I was not going to ever stop waiting for you. Somehow I knew in my heart you were near." The old man broke down and sat on the floor, too overtaken to stand any longer. "Get me some water, son."

Little Bear filled a cup with water and held it to the old man's lips.

"My wife did not tell me she was carrying you. In those days, before the reservation push, the Army wives came to live in the fort, or in the town of Fort Shaw. She wanted to be with me. We had plans of homesteading when I was to be relieved of duty."

Little Bear was having a hard time trying to understand the English. How he wished Eagle Feather was with him. He heard a noise; like a vision Eagle Feather stood at the entrance to the cave. Little Bear ran to him and pulled him inside.

"You followed me. You knew I'd come here. Help me now to hear this story."

Eagle Feather helped the old man to sit up. They recognized each other from the festival and the old man seemed content with his being there to translate what he had to say to the boy.

Eagle Feather spoke. "Little Bear, your mother is dead like Flower Woman told you. Her body was never found. This man is your father in the white man's world. You were raised the Indian way."

Little Bear began to understand. "That is why I want to know about white man's ways. I will return to the school and work hard to learn the language. I will keep this in my heart." He put his hand on the old man's shoulder. "I will return to you and you can come to the fort. I am boarding at the Mission. We must learn about each other's ways." This was a lot for Little Bear to take in. He knew now why he had feelings for another way of life. He knew nothing about this other way; he was a reservation child.

"Yes. I will come to see you as soon as I am able. You asked me, what is your white man's name? It is, from this day forward…Thomas."

Little Bear and Eagle Feather left the cave, mounted their horses and, once again, as if by magic, disappeared before the old man's eyes. At the top of the trail, Eagle Feather turned back; Little Bear turned forward.

44

WINTER STRUCK EARLY dumping two feet of snow, drifting in the powerful winds up to six feet high along the fence lines. People stayed home; school days were filled with reading assignments to keep the students active and motivated. A few Indians left and returned to their tribes. But Little Bear progressed at a rapid pace. He was so hungry for this other world of surprises that he put aside his personal problems.

He completed two years of classwork that first year at the Mission. Now it was spring and tests were going to prove his abilities. If he passed the tests, he could advance to another school for higher education. He started to worry about this in the beginning of March when the snow turned into rain and the ice left the river allowing it to flow freely once again.

The spring day in May held so much happiness and excitement Little Bear thought his heart would burst, if not his head. He spoke fluent English; wrote long essays; a few letters to his Blackfoot family; knew his numbers, and visited with the blackrobes about his future.

"Little Bear don't worry so much. You will make yourself ill." Father Jerome was both pleased and concerned with Little Bear's progress. "Do you still want to go to the Carlisle Indian Industrial School in Pennsylvania?"

"Yes. More than ever. I want to become a lawyer. There will be a need for an advocate for the Indian tribes in a few years. I could serve as an Indian representative in the courts. My background from living in Montana Territory would be important for this work."

"Then here is the plan. Send in the forms you have kept all these years. Father Michael and I will be leaving this mission, assigned to a new Diocese by this coming fall. We will go together to this school." He looked around the room. "Father Michael probably will be given an easy assignment and be semi-retired. As of now, I do not know my fate. Our order of priests has a seminary in Pennsylvania. It is as if the Good Lord is guiding us once again. It will be hard for me to leave here."

"I will be eighteen before fall. They will not turn me down." I would like a visit with my family before we leave."

"Granted. Now, let's get this graduation certificate signed and you can march in a procession with the other graduates. Out the door with you."

The forms were mailed that next day. In three weeks they were returned marked 'accepted'. Little Bear rode his horse to visit his Indian family.

"Flower Woman, my Mother, and Bear Chief, my father." He greeted them in the traditional way. "I am here with news. I am leaving with the blackrobes for more school."

He smiled at Flower Woman. "I have a request. "Cut my hair the white man way. Keep my braids with your medicine bag. I will take some hair for my bag. Put some in Wise Owl's bag. Give Eagle Feather my hair tied with a beaded bracelet that you made. He can put it with his warrior shirt. I want a strand to give to Old Man Who Lives In The Cave. He has a huge trunk full of his memories."

"When do you leave?"

"I want to talk to Eagle Feather, and to Wise Owl, and to Looking Back. I want to thank them for watching over me like spirit guides."

"We will have a ceremony."

"I will give my address and information to Eagle Feather. He will know how to find me if you need me. I will write you."

Father Jerome was surprised to see Little Bear so soon. "What happened to your hair?"

"One of the requirements of the school is we have our hair cut short.

I didn't want them to cut it and toss it into a fire. My hair is to be buried with me. It is part of my body. Another school rule is we cannot speak the Indian language to any other student; only English." He thought a minute then said, "Their goal is to ready us for the dominant society of the white man." He laughed. "My name back there will be Thomas." He smiled at Father Jerome. "I would like to take your name 'Jerome' for my last name on the forms for the rest of my life."

"Why Thomas, that is quite an honor for me. I am very proud of you and your determination to advance with your new life. Yes. You may use my name whenever it is necessary." They shook hands. "I've always wanted a son and now you have three dads."

He pulled Little Bear into a big bear hug and he said a prayer of protection over his new namesake. "You came back without your horse. Why?"

I said goodby to my faithful mount and left him where he was meant to be. He was gifted to me by Bear Chief when I first came here. Bear Chief will take care of him for me."

Little Bear stopped talking for a second. "The horse I came back on maybe Mary Fields could use. Would you find out for me?"

"Of course. She is living in Cascade now and I am sure she would love to have your horse. Her café is full all the time, but she forgets to give them a bill when they leave. She has such a generous soul and will not be able to keep that pace much longer. I heard she is going to take in laundry if the café folds."

"We will be on our way after a few more matters are settled here at the Mission."

"Will we go by wagon?"

The priest laughed. "No. The world is a busy place and we will go on the Iron Horse. It is called a train. We will sleep many nights on this train and have a few rest stops along the way."

One of our first and very important stops will be for us to go shopping for clothes for you. You will have to get used to wearing tight fitting trousers, vests and shoes that will pinch your toes. It will be my graduation gift to you. I started a bank account when I first came into

Montana Territory hoping for just such an occasion as what you are presenting."

———◆◆◆◆———

Martha and her son, Tom drove them to the train depot. As usual it was running late.

Martha had a basket full of homemade breads, jams, cheeses, boiled eggs, and fancy deserts. The basket was so heavy the bottom almost tore loose when Father Michael took it from her.

"Martha, how about one last blessing for you and your family? Maybe you could make a sampler wall hanging to remember us by?"

"I'll do it, Father. Just say the words."

Thank you Lord for placing this lovely woman into our lives. Give her health and happiness and a bit of wealth to go with it. In Jesus' name. Amen."

Just then the train came blowing steam and its whistle.

"Goodby you dear men. If you ever are out our way…" Martha had to stop talking. She grabbed her son's arm, pulled out her lace hankie and waved until the train went around a corner and all she could see was a trail of black smoke being carried by the ever blowing wind.

Little Bear sat in an empty seat near a window. He watched the fields of spring; saw newborn calves hopping over each other. He had not thought it would be so hard to say goodbye to everything he loved and knew. After a few miles he reached up and pulled down the gray shade.

———◆◆◆◆———

45

BY THE TIME Martha's basket was empty the train had reached their destination. The new surroundings were confusing at first since Little Bear had never dreamed of what a civilized dominant society would be like. Father Jerome checked with his order to announce his arrival. He and Father Michael had a private moment, promising to stay in touch. Almost twenty years of friendship would not be severed.

Little Bear had decided to use his white man name, Thomas Jerome, the minute he landed in the Pennsylvania train station.

Their next excursion included a buggy ride through the mansion district. This came as a total shock to Little Bear. People live in those big houses with beautiful flowers and trees and fences. I wonder what the houses look like inside? How could they possibly have enough chairs and beds to fill the rooms? Maybe someday I'll live in a house like that three story white one that has all the trimmings on the roof line. I wonder why that is up there? What possibly could it do to make the house warmer or stronger? Oh, I have so much to learn.

The buggy driver pulled up in front of the Carlisle Indian School and Father Jerome and Thomas climbed out. Father had coin to pay the man. They walked up the stairs and went in without knocking on the front door. Little Bear was not ready for what he saw. He kept twirling in circles soaking in all the pillars holding up ceilings over 20 feet high. Special art work captured his imagination when he saw Indian paintings done by past students of the school.

He stared at the prettiest girl he had ever seen. She smiled back from behind her desk.

"Welcome. May I help you?" Her bright blue eyes sparkled and she displayed a friendly warmness in her voice. Little Bear had never seen a white woman wear her hair in a coil; the result was like staring at a brightly shining crown atop massive curls around her face.

Father Jerome made the introductions. Little Bear was tongue tied. The girl stood there blushing at the handsome young man.

"Ahem!" A voice broke the spell. "We are here to enroll Thomas Jerome. Can you tell us where to go for that?"

The young woman snapped out of her fantasy. "I can help you with that." She asked for the forms and Father Jerome handed over the crumpled up papers. She checked for signatures and did not act surprised at the condition of the forms. She assigned Little Bear his room number and pointed down the long hallway.

"Go out that door at the end of the hall. You will see a barracks with numbers over the door. Enter through that door and you will find your room." She handed Little Bear a key. "This land used to be a government fort. Now it is growing every year.

In fact, we are very well known for sports." She looked at the two men standing in front of her. Have you heard of Jim Thorpe? Probably not, seeing where you come from. He is a star graduate of our school. He won all kinds of gold medals in the Olympic games."

Now it was official. Thomas Jerome for the first time in his life was strictly on his own. He felt chills. Was he frightened or elated? Only time would tell. They carried his bags through the barracks door, found his room and Thomas turned the key.

Father Jerome held out his hand to Little Bear. "You have my address. If you need anything get word to me. I will check in on you occasionally. Study hard and do us proud."

◆◆◆◆◆

Little Bear adapted to the school, rapidly advancing in his studies. The four school years passed quickly; it seemed to blur in his mind.

He lay on his cot looking at the ceiling where a fan whirled trying to cool the air. *Can it possibly be my college graduation day? I hope Father Jerome and Father Michael will be in the audience.* They were. So was the fair maiden who had checked him in over four years ago. He saw her and grinned as he walked by in his purple gown and silly board hat. He had earned a gold tassel for his grades and it kept flipping into his left eye. It still seemed like a dream when he thought about his actual graduation as a lawyer, now a grown man with a purpose. He felt a shock in his finger tips when the college president handed him the lambskin document. He officially carried the title as a lawyer, and could try to make a difference in the lives of his Indian family.

The next day after the graduation ceremony, Little Bear packed his meager belongings, anxious to leave the school. He patted his suit vest pocket, assuring himself that his ticket was safe. The walk to the train station would clear his brain and he looked forward to the jaunt.

———•—•—•———

A soft knock brought him back to the reality of the day. When he opened the door he stared at the smiling eyes and could not hold back his surprise at seeing his visitor. There stood the girl of his dreams, the school receptionist.

"Come in, come in. What brings you to my door?" He backed into the room and Ingrid did not hesitate to follow him. "Here. Sit on this chair. I'm sorry I don't have any tea to offer you."

Ingrid primly sat on the little wicker chair and folded her arms into her lap. Her blonde hair neatly combed into a braided bun. "I...I wanted to see you before you left tomorrow." She reached into her satchel and removed a paper. "I hope you don't think I am being too bold." She dropped her eyes to stare at her shoes. "I have written my name and address on this paper and I am hoping you will write me." She looked up at Little Bear with such love shining in her sparkling blue eyes that he blushed.

"Oh! Yes. I will write you as soon as I find a place to live in

Washington. Thank you for being so thoughtful. I had planned to stop by your desk."

"Would you ever come to Washington on a visit now that the war has settled down and trains are traveling in safety once again?" He folded the paper and put it in his vest pocket.

Ingrid smiled and lit up the room.

"Yes, in fact, I have applied for a different type of employment in Washington. My office skills are sharp and the politicians are always in need of secretaries who know shorthand and how to type. Perhaps we will see each other often?" She blushed.

Thomas smiled and took her hand. "I would like that very much. I will write a letter recommending you." I don't have an address to give back to you, but as soon as I do, you will hear from me. In the meantime, I'll be hunting for room and board for you as well as for myself."

Ingrid jumped up from the chair and gracefully walked to the still open door. She turned, smiled, waved and was gone.

Did I just dream the most wonderful dream? Little Bear patted his vest pocket and felt the folded paper. *Ah! My next adventure is about to begin.*

He had accepted the job offered to him with the large firm in Washington. They are working on Peace Treaties with the Indian tribes settled all over this country. I have an understanding about this and will be a great benefit for the firm. Besides, they will pay me well and I can begin to live the white man's idea of being successful.

Little Bear, aka Thomas Jerome, stepped through the dormitory door for the last time. He locked the door without a final look back.

46

T HE LANDSCAPE FROM the train window was a wonderful sight in the bright daylight. He went quickly to the address of his employer. He was excited to start his first day. He signed a form officially changing his name from Little Bear to Thomas Jerome. He wanted to take the name of "Thomas" the man in the cave had given him years ago. Without hesitation he wrote the name "Jerome" for his sir name in honor of Father Jerome.

Little Bear wrote in his journal all about the changes he was experiencing.

It is both frightening and exhilarating. I am now a lawyer.
I live and work in a very busy city called Washington.
It is still recovering from the battles of the Civil War.
My world is expanded beyond belief.
I have not seen Flower Woman and Bear Chief for
four years. My plan is to visit next spring.
When I have an address, I'll send it to Eagle Feather. Maybe
I can set up a tipi on the capitol lawn?
It is hard for me to imagine them as elders.

He also wrote to Eagle Feather and after stretching his legs and pulling on his fingers, he once again dipped his quilled pen into the ink bottle. He wanted to write to Father Jerome as well. Neither letter would be mailed until he had an address to send to the men. *I must find a boarding house near the capitol soon. The graduation money from the two priests will not last long in this very expensive city. Ah! Tomorrow I'll find just the place.*

Thomas left the hotel after eating a very large breakfast from a buffet table set up each morning for paying guests. He pulled his coat tighter around his neck, and stepped briskly down the street toward the government office building.

"Well, would you look at that sign? He stopped and stared at the stately two-storied house with gingerbread trim. The sign in the window said "**Rooms for Rent.**"

Thomas quickly released the strap holding the spiked iron gate shut and stepped through the opening. He walked the few short steps, reached for the doorbell twist knob on the middle panel and waited. An elderly gray-haired woman, wearing a clean white apron, swung open the door.

I'm here to inquire about your sign in the window." Thomas pointed to the sign. "I am new to this city, working for the Government. I have good references if you need them. I'm single, and a lawyer. I need a place to live and this fits my needs. I want to walk to work each morning."

"Come in, young man. Get out of that cold wind blowing today." She stepped aside and Thomas walked into another world of white man's style and culture. "Set your briefcase there by the door and follow me." She pointed down a hallway to a stairway. "I'll show you what you can rent for five dollars a week. If you want meals, that cost will be twenty-five cents for breakfast and fifty cents for the evening meal." She smiled and took a breath. Her hand crossed over her heart as she told him she did not have any renters presently.

"Well, I can help you out with that. I will sign on for both room and board starting tonight. And, I have a friend moving here soon. So… you will have two room-and-boarders by the end of this month."

"My name is Mrs. Cochrane. I am a widow and I don't want pets here."

"That is fine with me. I will be working many late hours and won't have time to dog walk."

Mrs. Cochrane raised one eye brow as she walked him into the parlor where she had a lengthy shelf filled with books. A large bay window covered with delicate lace panels gave off a soft glow from the now-risen sun. In front of the curtains stood a delicate wood table that held an Edison phonograph machine. Thomas had never seen one and he planned to ask Mrs. Cochrane what it was and how did she make it work. A chess set and a checkers board filled the square marble top on the small table in the corner. Horse-hair-covered soft chairs filled empty space along the north wall. "You are welcome to spend quiet nights in this room with other boarders. However, lights out by 9 P.M. most nights.

"Anything else I need to know?"

"Well, no smoking in your room, no drinking or cussing, and absolutely no women in your room." She turned away and walked toward the front door. "I will give you a key when you return."

"No problem, Mrs. Cochrane." He looked at his pocket watch. "I must get to work on time." Thomas picked up his briefcase and left through the same door he had entered. He whistled the rest of his walk, spoke cheerfully to the receptionist on the main floor, and asked her to bring him a cup of hot coffee. When she reappeared he handed her a greenback bill and asked her to bring him back coins.

By noon-time, Thomas was a bundle of nerves. He hurried out the massive doors and looked for a telephone booth set up on many of the street corners. He spotted what he was looking for and hurried, walking against the wind, to make his telephone call to Ingrid.

"Hello? Hello?" Ingrid jiggled her receiver hoping for a better connection. The candlestick style of telephone was light weight and easy to use.

"Ingrid. It's me. Thomas. I've great news." He put the mouth piece close and shouted. "Ingrid. I've found a boarding house. Come as soon as you can." He heard Ingrid's laughter. "Thomas. Is this really you? You found a place so soon?"

"Yes! It is just what we need. Two separate floors, breakfast and dinner…" He paused to catch his breath. "Send me a telegram when you have made your travel plans. I'll meet you. We can walk to the government building, and it is a charming old home filled with the landlady's precious items."

A voice cut in on the line. "You must end this call, sir, or deposit another coin."

"Goodbye for now Ingrid." Thomas hung up the phone on the hook inside the box.

47

Mrs. Cochrane opened the door when she heard Thomas scraping the gate. She had spent some time preparing a nice evening supper for the two of them.

"Good evening, Mrs. Cochrane. Uum! Something smells mighty fine coming from your kitchen." Thomas was in a festive mood, even after lugging his simple belongings from the hotel room to this house. He went to the wash room and washed his hands and splashed cool water onto his beard, drying it with a towel laid out for him. He then went into the kitchen where Mrs. Cochrane waited. She had hot floured biscuits with honey on a plate, and while she bid Thomas to sit, she ladled up a very large bowl of beef and vegetables. She poured him a cup of very strong coffee and offered him fresh, thick cream. Thomas didn't realize how hungry he was for a good, home cooked meal like this. "This is very good, Mrs. Cochrane. If you cook for me every night like this I'll need to buy me larger sized clothes."

Eventually Mrs. Cochrane brought up the payment schedule. Thomas paid her for both rooms and figured out how much his meals would be per week. She smiled when she saw the coins spilling out of a pouch from a vest pocket.

"I talked to my friend and plans are being made for an arrival before too many more days." Thomas stood up. He had unpacking to do and he was tired from a long day.

"What time is breakfast? I have to be at work by ten o'clock each morning and it takes me about 20 minutes to walk the distance."

Mrs. Cochrane smiled. "I'm up early. We can plan for eight o'clock tomorrow and see how that works for us." She looked about her kitchen. "Ham and eggs and toast and jam should fill you up. Coffee is always on the stove, back space."

Thomas laughed, and thanked her again for the meal.

Now to test out that lovely iron frame bed…I wonder if it has goose down pillows and mattress. Life is wonderful and all I see is good. He untied one boot and kicked out his foot. *I'm needing some socks darned. I wonder if Mrs. Cochrane does sewing.*

————◆—◆◆—◆—◆————

I must write Father Jerome tomorrow with news of my good fortune. Without him none of this would be happening. Thomas fell asleep a happy man. When the sun filled the window with its bright light it startled him. But the wonderful smell of ham frying in the kitchen had him scurrying to dress. *I'm ready for a hot cup of that very dark coffee Mrs. Cochrane likes.*

In all of his excitement, Thomas forgot it was Saturday. He would have the whole day to get properly settled. *I wonder if there is a shed out in back where I can store my satchel and outdoor boots and gear.*

Breakfast came and went but not without more surprises. A Western Union Telegraph delivery boy, riding the typical bicycle, rang its' bell announcing he had a telegram for Thomas.

The message was from Ingrid.

Thomas. Stop.

Meet the train Today, Saturday, at 4 P.M. Stop.

Bring a wagon. Stop.

I have a trunk and two satchels. Stop.

Ingrid. Stop

Thomas hurried to tell Mrs. Cochrane the good news. He was shocked to find her frowning, not dancing around in the kitchen. Her hands were wrapped in her long apron pinned to her shoulders. "You didn't tell me you were going to live with a young woman. I am very disappointed in you." She sat on a high stool by the dry sink.

"Does it matter?" I didn't think to mention it because Ingrid is my sister and I guess I never thought about her being a girl. But, I assure you, she is a very decent young woman. She is educated to do office work and excited about being a government employee." Thomas looked very sorrowful at the older woman. "Please give her a chance. If you don't like her living here, then I'll find someplace else for us to live." He looked to the floor. "This house is perfect for our needs and is such a charming home for you. Why, Ingrid would even help you keep the dust out."

Mrs. Cochrane frowned, put her index finger to her cheek and decided Ingrid could be a good thing. "Bring the young lady here. We can give it a try. I need the money and you two will be stable renters."

Thomas took a deep breath and slowly released the air, like a little boy playing with a balloon. "Thank you. I can help you with repairs and things, too."

With that settled, Thomas went to his room. He wanted to finish his letter to Eagle Feather.

Dear Eagle Feather,

Some time has gone by since my last letter. I have so much news. It is both frightening and exhilarating. I am now a lawyer. I live and work in a very busy city called Washington. It is still recovering from the battles of the Civil War. My world is expanded beyond belief.

As you know, I have not seen Flower Woman and Bear Chief for many years. Not a day goes by that I don't think of you all.

My plan is to visit next spring after the snows leave the fields and travel can be arranged. Trains are running across the plains and travel is safe once again.

I have met a wonderful woman who is curious about my past. My plan is to ask her to marry me and we can make a trip to the Reservation. Hopefully, things are much better now since the Government has been working in Congress to help with new Treaties.

Peace,
Little Bear.

Thomas placed the letter to Father Jerome alongside the letter meant for Eagle Feather. He placed his eye glasses and watch on the dresser drawer top.

48

THOMAS HAD SOME difficulty in locating and hiring a wagon-cab at the train station. He walked the long distance and arrived a little ahead of time in order to not be flushed when he saw Ingrid.

"Thomas. Thomas. Come this way. I'm over here." He turned to face her and she gave him a big hug. "This is really happening?" Her smile lit up the area. He grabbed her hand and they dashed off to the freight car to wait for the wagon and for help in loading the trunk.

"Ingrid. What have you hidden in that trunk? Everything you own?"

"Well, I need everything I brought. Besides I couldn't leave anything at the school room I rented for the past four years." She touched her hat with hand covered gloves.

Ingrid showed delight in every building the driver took them past until she saw the government building off to her left. "Oh…oh…I do so want to work there." She clapped her hands together, overtaken with fresh emotion.

Thomas smiled. 'Driver, turn here, into the alley side of the house."

Mrs. Cochrane stood in the doorway wearing her usual apron. He noticed a young man standing alongside of her and his heart fell. Had she rented the room instead of waiting for Ingrid?

"Welcome to my home, young lady. I have a supper ready and this fellow, (she gave the younger man a shove) Joe, is going to help you unload that trunk and bring it into the house. Thomas pay the cabbie and let's get on with it."

Mrs. Cochrane had instantly fallen for this lovely young woman who was so eager to help out, and do chores needing to be done. Thomas decided it was time to tell the truth about Ingrid.

He knew he couldn't keep lying to this woman who trusted them both to be in her home.

He hadn't even told Ingrid about the fabrication.

Supper was a simple cornbread and honey mixture with slices of ham and baked beans. Green lettuce washed and sprinkled with a bit of sugar put it all together and instead of coffee, Mrs. Cochrane had made sweet tea drinks. Thomas clinked the side of his glass.

"Please, I have something to say. First of all, this meal was delicious and you must share your recipe with Ingrid. She will be making her own recipe book starting any time soon." He looked at Ingrid and smiled. "Mrs. Cochrane, I have a confession to make to you. I lied to you when I told you Ingrid was my sister." He heard a strange noise coming from the older woman.

"I have known Ingrid for over 4 years and when I left college I left her behind. It was then I discovered I am in love with her. When she told me she wanted to come to Washington to work for the government I could think of nothing better than for the two of us to be together in this big rushing city." Thomas paused and took a drink of water. The women remained seated, silent in their thoughts.

"I want to marry you Ingrid. I love you and promise to give you a good life as my wife."

Thomas knelt on one knee and placed his hands into Ingrid's. He felt her trembling. *Wow! Now I've done it.*

Ingrid stared at Thomas for what seemed an eternity. "It is about time you spoke up for me. Of course I want to be your wife. From the first time you walked into that school lobby I knew I'd wait for this moment, however long it took."

Mrs. Cochrane pulled out her handkerchief from her apron pocket and took a swipe at her eyes before she blew her nose. "Looks like only good is coming our way. You will want to continue living here after you marry won't you?" She put her hands in her lap. "I can't imagine you moving away from me so soon."

"Ingrid walked over to the woman and put her arms around her neck. "Thank you for understanding. We have a wedding to plan, simple as it will be. Maybe you could teach me how to sew a nice dress for the occasion?"

49

I N LESS THAN two weeks a rather battered looking envelope arrived for Little Bear. An office secretary dropped the envelope on Thomas' desktop. It was from Eagle Feather.

"How come this is addressed to an Indian named Little Bear? Is that someone you know here in Washington?"

"It's a long story, meant for another day. Thank you for delivering it to me."

Thomas sat staring at the letter. He had read it over and over, still not fully comprehending. The post mark said Browning, Montana Territory. One sheet of white lined paper folded over three times fit snugly into the envelope. It was addressed to Little Bear. Beneath that was printed c/o: Thomas Jerome. Attorney at Law; Esq. He noticed it had taken over three months for the letter to reach him. Little Bear slid a letter-opener knife under the sealed flap. *This letter crossed paths with my letter. The Great Spirit must have messages for us.* Eagle Feather had neatly formed the words of the first sentence; first in Blackfoot marks, and then in white man's words.

HOKAHAY! Bear Chief is ill. The reservation doctors have no remedy; Our Medicine Man has no remedy; The drummers have no power to relieve his pain. By the time this letter reaches you he will be following the Grizzly Bear. That path will be lit by torches; his feet dressed in beaded moccasins Flower Woman makes. He did not ask me to write, but we talked. He said you were found barely alive. You were rescued by Wise Owl. He bonded to you in a blood brother way. He guided you; saw to it you were raised in the Blackfoot tradition. Wise Owl kept the vow to Bear Chief to keep you a secret. Always know Bear Chief is proud of you. He loves you. He has the spirit of peace. The blackrobe here baptized Bear Chief into the faithful Christian's tribe two moons ago. Wise Owl protects Flower Woman and Looking Back. I soon will be the next chief. It is his wish that I follow in my brother's earthly footsteps. There will never be another great Bear Chief. I will honor his memory.

Eagle Feather

Shocked by this message, Little Bear pondered what to do. *I must make arrangements to go to my family. Bear Chief lives no more?* He scribbled a few words on note paper to give to his secretary to start the plans for his trip.

He heard a knock at his office door and looked up to see three Blackfoot Indians. Dressed in western style clothes each man held a Stetson hat in front of him.

"Yes? Can I help you?"

In broken English the middle man, apparently the leader, spoke.

"We come to see Little Bear. The Great Spirit sends us to find him."

——•——•◆•——•◆•——•◆•——•——